But right now he wanted to get Rikki out of here. They were too exposed at this location.

She finally nodded. "I need to get my things."

After he escorted her to her room, he put her in his car and turned to stare at her. "Where to, princess?"

She swallowed, dropped her head and stared at her hands in her lap. "The Bay Road."

Bay Road? Blain whistled. Real estate out there was way over his pay scale. "Okay, then."

Pricey estates out there. A scenic highway surrounding where the big bay met up with Millbrook River and the lake.

When they were under way and out past the city, he turned off and followed the dark water. "What's the address?"

She finally looked over at him, a defiance in her voice. "2200 First Bay Lane."

Blain blinked, thinking he hadn't heard right. "Hey, that's—"

"The Alvanetti estate," she finished for him.
"Sonia Alvanetti is my mother."

"And...Franco Alvanetti is your father."

"Yes." She nodded and looked out the window.

And suddenly Blain understood so much more about what was going on with Rikki Allen. No wonder she'd been so closemouthed and evasive. No wonder he couldn't trust her.

She was an Alvanetti.

Lenora Worth writes award-winning romance and romantic suspense. Three of her books finaled in the ACFW Carol Awards, and her Love Inspired Suspense novel *Body of Evidence* became a *New York Times* bestseller. Her novella in *Mistletoe Kisses* made her a *USA TODAY* bestselling author. With sixty books published and millions in print, she goes on adventures with her retired husband, Don, and enjoys reading, baking and shopping...especially shoe shopping.

Books by Lenora Worth

Love Inspired Suspense

Men of Millbrook Lake

Her Holiday Protector

Capitol K-9 Unit

Proof of Innocence

Fatal Image
Secret Agent Minister
Deadly Texas Rose
A Face in the Shadows
Heart of the Night
Code of Honor
Risky Reunion
Assignment: Bodyguard
The Soldier's Mission
Body of Evidence
The Diamond Secret
Lone Star Protector
In Pursuit of a Princess
Forced Alliance
Deadly Holiday Reunion

Visit the Author Profile page at Harlequin.com for more titles.

HER HOLIDAY PROTECTOR

LENORA WORTH

HARLEQUIN LOVE INSPIRED® SUSPENSE

Recycling programs
for this product may
not exist in your area.

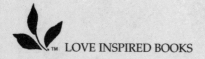

™ LOVE INSPIRED BOOKS

ISBN-13: 978-0-373-67707-8

Her Holiday Protector

www.Harlequin.com

Printed in U.S.A.

But let justice roll on like a river,
righteousness like a never-failing stream!
—Amos 5:24

To Winnie Griggs, Beth Cornelison and Renee Ryan
With gratitude for a wonderful retreat during a storm

ONE

The sickle moon dipped down in the dark sky, reaching toward the gray surface of Millbrook Lake like a slinky hand trying to touch the water. The nip of winter covered the dusk in a crisp, fresh-smelling blanket of evening dew.

Blain Kent inhaled a deep, cleansing breath and hit his stride on the path around the big oval lake, the cadence of his nightly run echoing behind him. All around him, the quaint turn-of-the-century houses shone with pretty white lights and fresh evergreen wreaths tied up with bright red bows.

Christmas had come to Northwest Florida. But tonight, Blain had to work off that big Thanksgiving meal he'd enjoyed at his parents' house two days ago. He also needed to work off his retired law enforcement father's always critical comments. Blain might have followed in his father's footsteps by returning from combat to take a job with the Millbrook Police Department, but that was where the similarities ended.

Serving for over twenty-five years in the sheriff's department and finally becoming the county sheriff, Sam Kent had tried to keep the peace by pandering to the local elite and turning a blind eye on the powerful Alvanetti crime family that tried to run the entire state of Florida. *Alleged* crime family since no one could ever pin anything illegal on Franco Alvanetti.

While Blain tried to do an honest day's work and solve crimes by the book, it irritated him to no end that he couldn't find a single piece of incriminating evidence on the Alvanetti clan. So Blain and his still-influential father had a difference of opinion on which way worked best. Blain didn't pander to anyone.

Blain rounded a corner, his thoughts centered on the harsh words he and his father had slung at each other while Mom was in the kitchen dishing up pumpkin pie.

"Don't be so hard on yourself or anyone else around here," Dad had said in his deep, disapproving voice. "You have to make it work, son. Don't make waves. Just keep the peace."

"I want it to work, Dad. For everyone, not just the rich people who live around the lake and out on the canal."

Blain approached that canal now, out of habit

his cop's gaze taking in his surroundings. He wouldn't let that conversation with his father ruin his good mood. Not tonight, with that moon hanging over the lake and the whole world alive with the promise of something true and honest around the bend. Christmas was coming. All would be right with the world.

And then he heard a gunshot followed a few seconds later by a woman's scream.

Blain's radar went into overdrive. He glanced up and down the narrow part of the lake that met up with the Millbrook River. On both sides of the canal, town houses and apartment buildings lined the way. Blain stopped, listening, his gaze sweeping the left side of the river, where the footpath turned into a boardwalk along the row of houses. Footbridges connected both sides, most high enough for large boats to pass underneath.

Where had the gunshot and scream come from?

Maybe a car had backfired but he knew a gunshot when he heard one and the scream had definitely been real. He heard footfalls coming toward him. Blain wasn't carrying his weapon, but he waited, anyway. He knew how to defend himself.

A small figure came running up the boardwalk. As the silhouette came nearer, he grew even more concerned.

A woman. She sprinted toward him, her long dark hair flying out behind her like a lacy shawl. She kept glancing back as if she were running away from someone.

"Ma'am, are you hurt?"

She came to a surprised stop and drew to a halt a few feet away from him, fear radiating off her body.

"I… I need help," she said on a shaky voice, her breathing shallow. "Someone was inside my house when I got home and… I think they shot my friend."

"I'm a police officer," he said to calm her. "Stay there. I'll walk toward you."

She searched behind her and then turned back, her expression full of fear and doubt. "How do I know you're telling the truth?"

Blain tugged his badge out of the inside pocket of his hoodie and held it up so she could see it in the street light's glow. "See? Millbrook Police Department."

When the woman frowned and backed away, he said, "Just relax. I won't hurt you. Have you called 911?"

"No. I just got out of there," she said again, glancing back behind her. "I need…your help.

Someone was in my house. I heard them, saw them in my backyard."

"Okay, I'm here." He walked closer, his badge in one hand and the other hand out so she could see it. "What happened to you?"

"It's not me," she said, her dark eyes flashing. "It's my friend Tessa." She pointed, flinging her arm back behind her. "I… I think she's dead. I mean, I know she's dead. I found her there after I heard a gunshot outside my back door. I… I ran out and saw a man running away."

Blain's instincts kicked in. A murder in Millbrook. That was something he rarely had to deal with. "Show me. Can you take me to your place? I can check on your friend and check your house. And we'll call for backup, too."

The woman nodded, pushed at her hair, her dark eyes going black. "Yes. She's…she's at my town house. Up there."

She motioned toward the end of the long canal to a prime spot of real estate on the corner. Nice for sunsets and enjoying the channel that opened up into the lake and river.

Blain clipped his badge on the outside pocket of his hoodie. "Okay, show me where you found the woman and let me check your house."

She waited, her hands fisted against a trim dark jacket. Blain came up beside her. "I'm Detective Blain Kent."

She didn't acknowledge that introduction but she did uncurl her fingers. Blain took the seconds ticking by to notice her hands and her face. No sign of a struggle and no visible wounds or any sign of blood. But she looked shocked and dazed. "What's your name?"

"Rikki."

Okay, Rikki who obviously didn't want to give out too much information right now.

He followed her between the narrow, two-storied houses, each one similar to the next except they were painted in various colors of pastel blues and yellows, mixed in with vivid whites. This new, swank development had the same Victorian flair as the turn-of-the-century homes along the lake. And came with a high price tag to match.

"I live here," she said, hurrying now as they approached a muted yellow townhome. "She's out on the patio."

She went through an open ornate gate decorated with a bright red-and-green wreath, but she stopped and took Blain's hand when he came up behind her.

A charge of awareness rushed up his arm, like a river wake rippling against the shore. Blain held to her, thinking how tiny her hand felt against his. He didn't argue or pull away.

She might bolt if he made a wrong move.

"There," she said with a gulp. "She comes to stay with me sometimes on weekends. I heard the shot when I came in the house and found her when I saw the back door open."

Blain took in the scene. A cedar wooden table overturned, a matching chair flipped over, its striped cushions lying against the brick surface of the spacious patio. He glanced from those items to the woman lying on her stomach against the redbrick, blood pooling all around her. Blain made his way to the woman, careful not to disturb anything. He knelt and checked her neck for a pulse.

None. Dead.

He stood and pulled out his phone.

"Is she…is she dead?"

He nodded to the obvious. "Yes. I have to call it in and I need to check inside."

"I'm going with you," the woman said, averting her gaze from the dead woman. "I… I heard someone and then I heard the gun go off. He shot her."

"Did you see him shoot her?"

"No. I came home and walked through the house. Then I heard the gunshot. He ran away when I screamed."

She was in shock, no doubt about that. "I need you to wait out here, okay? You can sit on the porch."

She nodded and allowed him to guide her to the small covered area where a white wrought-iron bistro set was hidden by a thick jasmine vine.

"I'm calling for backup and then I'll check the scene. Don't move from this spot."

"Okay." She leaned her elbows on the table and hung her head in her hands. "Hurry, please."

Blain went inside, all the while on the phone with dispatch. Nothing downstairs. Just a couple of open drawers and cabinets. He silently made his way upstairs where he found two bedrooms. Pretty much the same. A closet open and ransacked and some jewelry scattered on a dresser in what looked like the master bedroom. A purse dumped in the guest room.

After clearing the place, he came back outside. "I didn't find anyone else inside," he said to the woman.

He studied the scene while he explained things to the dispatcher. The woman had been shot in the back. Running away? Then he noticed where her right hand lay out from her body. The blood spatter there looked smeared with a pattern that looked like some sort of letter—a *K* with a line next to it. Interesting. He took a picture with his cell phone.

When he heard a soft moan, he turned to find

Rikki standing by the porch railing, her gaze caught on the dead woman.

She pivoted, a hand to her mouth. He could see her shoulders moving. He heard soft sobs. While he explained his location and the situation, he also noticed something else about the woman lying there on the cold brick.

She looked a lot like the woman standing there sobbing.

Rikki sat in a chair in the den while several police officers moved all around her. The Millbrook Police Department wasn't that big. Maybe three or four full-time officers and one very good-looking detective. She knew this because her family made it their business to keep up with the locals. But she'd been gone a few years and this new detective was different from the good ole boys she remembered.

He looked too intense and moody to bow down to anyone.

She took another gulp of air and closed her eyes to the scene she'd come home and found an hour ago. The house quiet, her cat gone, and the patio door open. Lights blinking away on the Christmas tree by the fireplace. Tessa? She'd called out, thinking her friend had gone out back, maybe had taken Pebble with her since the big, fluffy cat liked to lie across the patio floor bricks, warm from the setting sun. And then she'd looked up and heard a gun firing.

But when she'd hurried outside, the last rays of the sunset had shown with a bright clarity on Tessa lying there. Still. So still. Rikki had screamed and then she'd hurried to find her phone. But when she'd heard footsteps running away and saw a man in her yard, she'd bolted away. Ran like a coward, to what? Where had she been heading?

Away. She needed to get away. If anyone knew who she really was…

"Rikki?"

She whirled on her chair, her heartbeat drumming against her temples. "Yes?"

Blain Kent knelt in front of her, one hand on the arm of the high-backed floral chair, a notebook and ink pen in his other hand. "Is there anyone you can call? Can you stay someplace else tonight?"

Rikki wanted to laugh but she couldn't muster up the strength. She did straighten in the chair, her gaze grabbing onto his face. If she weren't so numb with fear and shock, she'd flirt with him. But she didn't want to flirt. She wanted to go back and walk in the door and see Tessa standing in the kitchen, waiting for their night out on the town in Pensacola. Dinner and conversation and maybe a little flirting. Just a little.

"Rikki? Miss Allen?"

"I'll be okay here."

"It might not be safe." He rocked back on his heels, his sweatpants stretching to accommodate his solid leg muscles. "Do you know of anyone who might want to harm Tessa Jones or you?"

"No." She closed her eyes and prayed for strength. "I… I left Tallahassee to get away for a while. I just broke up with my boyfriend."

The detective's eyes lit up at that statement. "How bad was the breakup?"

"Bad enough. But he doesn't know where I am."

"Right."

"Did you get a good look at the person?"

She tried to remember. "No. Just from behind. He had on dark clothes, like sweats and a cap. Tall. He was tall. With black running shoes."

"Okay, that's something to go on."

"I left her lying there. I was so scared."

He let that go but Rikki felt sure he'd ask her more on that subject later. Could Chad have done this? Was he that vicious, that cruel?

"Tell me more about Tessa Jones," the detective said.

Rikki swallowed the heaviness in her throat. "Tessa grew up in Georgia but she lives in Tallahassee. We went to college together."

"We'll be investigating her background but

if you can think of anything that might help us, tell me now."

His words had gone into what sounded like a firm command. He'd probably investigate Rikki's background, too. "Do you suspect me, Detective?"

His expression was as fluid and unreadable as a midnight ocean. "I'm just trying to put the pieces together." He studied his notes. "It looks like she tried to write something. I can't be sure, but…some of the blood pattern looks like the letter *K* with a line slashed through it."

Rikki's stomach roiled and almost revolted at that image. "I don't know. She calls me KK sometimes. Her nickname for me."

She lowered her head, hoping to stop the nausea.

"You need anything?"

She glanced up at his face, the five o'clock shadow making him look mysterious. "I'm fine."

"So why was Tessa here alone?"

"We were meeting here for the weekend to catch up. I travel a lot so I don't get up here very often." She glanced around, wondering how she'd ever feel safe here again. "I have clients in the area. Orders coming in for art and furnishings. I was on my way home. She knew where to find the key."

He studied her with an intense inky gaze that

left her rattled. "So you're here for work and to get away from Tallahassee and your ex-boyfriend."

"Yes."

"What's his name?"

"Chad Presley."

She looked out toward where the medical examiner was about to take away Tessa's cold body. Should she tell him the truth? Should she admit the things that would cause him to suspect her of all kinds of crimes? Or should she sit here like a lump and pretend her life wasn't falling apart?

"Miss Allen? You said you came here to get away from him?"

Rikki lifted her head, her gaze slamming into his. Did he already have her figured out? "Yes, and to take care of some clients in the area and mostly, for a visit with my mother."

No, she'd covered all of her bases on that a long time ago. No one could figure her out. She should be safe.

But here she was, back in the one town she'd sworn she'd never return to again. For oh, so many reasons.

"Why did you need to get away from your ex?"

She didn't want to talk about Chad. "We've been apart for a while but he's having a hard time letting go. I just wanted some time away, to think about things."

"So you came here. Not that far away."

She bobbed her head. "My mother is sick," she said, sincerity her only hope. "I came to visit her during the holidays. I don't get back here too often."

"And who's your mother? Maybe you could go and stay with her?"

Rikki knew she'd said the wrong thing by the way he analyzed her with that deep blue-eyed stare.

She tried to fix it. "Can I just stay here? I'll lock up."

She didn't really want to stay here but she couldn't let him see how scared she felt right now. He already suspected her and…she couldn't explain anything else to him. The detective would jump to the wrong conclusions.

He gave up and stood. Rikki stood up, too, relieved that he wasn't so close to her anymore and that he seemed willing to let it go. For now.

But he didn't let it go.

"I don't think you should be alone right now, and you can't stay here, anyway. This is a crime scene."

"And I can't stay here because you think I'm in shock or because I'm a suspect or because you think whoever did this will be back?"

"All of the above," he said, not even blinking.

"I see." She moved away from him, her arms in a protective stance across her midsection. If she told him the truth, he would take her in for questioning. That's how things worked in her family. "I... I don't want to upset my mother."

"Then go to a hotel but as I said, this is a crime scene, so you can't get back in here until we've cleared it."

Rikki whirled to stare over at him and tried again. "I can't stay in my own home?"

"Not tonight."

His tone told her not to argue. "Okay, I'll find somewhere else." And she'd have to leave again. Soon. She'd go by to see her mother and then... she'd just go.

"Do you think your boyfriend followed you?"

"No."

She'd found someone in her house and they'd gotten away after killing Tessa. Instincts told her this wasn't Chad's doings, no matter how much he'd threatened her.

"Do you know anyone here besides your mother?"

She did, but no one she could trust. "No. I've been away for a while and as I said, I don't get back much."

He jotted notes. "I could drive you somewhere."

Rikki looked up at him to make sure he wasn't

trying to trip her up. Were detectives always this accommodating? "I have my car."

She turned away, her mind on the horrible scene outside the window. And where was Pebble? Where was her cat that traveled with her?

She refused to think about that or the tough-guy detective giving her the third degree. He probably already had her license plate number. Probably had already run it through the system.

He wouldn't find anything incriminating on Rikki Allen. But he could find a whole lot of information on Regina Alvanetti. Then he'd know she was the daughter of the infamous Franco Alvanetti.

"What do you want to do?" he asked, his tone telling her she didn't have much choice in making that decision.

"I want to cooperate with you," she said, resolve settling over her like the night chill. "But honestly, I'm not sure what to do next."

TWO

"I suggest you let me drive you somewhere safe."

Rikki turned to stare at up Blain with dark-chocolate eyes. "And where in this town would that be right now, Detective?"

Surprised, he said, "Well, Millbrook is pretty tame, all things considered. Preferably, with someone you trust. But I guess anywhere you want to go as long as you let me get you there and make sure it looks safe."

"I don't see why that's necessary."

Something was so not right here. Blain hadn't dealt with a murder case since returning to Millbrook after his stint as a marine MP. He'd worked hard serving his country and after doing recon work to track down some of the meanest humans on earth, he'd learned a thing or two about people. They tended to be evasive when they were trying hard to appear normal. Evasive and not so good at faking it.

This beautiful, frightened woman was definitely hiding something but he had to give her credit for staying fairly calm during this whole thing. Had she had a lot of practice?

He watched her pace, saw her glance out to where her friend had died. She was as nervous as her missing cat probably was right now, but she held it in check with a gritty silence. Natural, since she'd come home to find an intruder and her friend murdered. But why wasn't she opening up to him? Especially about the ex-boyfriend. A case of domestic abuse?

And why didn't this scene make any sense? A robbery? A random act? A revenge killing? What? And what was the victim trying to tell him? He had pictures of the whole scene and he'd study them later. Especially that possible letter *K* written in blood.

He tried a new tactic. "You know, you and the deceased look a lot alike."

She whirled at that, long ribbons of dark hair curling around her face and shoulders. "People told us that all through college. Said we looked like sisters. Tessa is…was…a year younger than me. I never imagined she wouldn't make it past twenty-eight."

So that made Rikki Allen twenty-nine, obviously.

Just a few years younger than him. Blain

cleared his head and got back on track. "Look, I'm the only detective in town and since I was first on the scene, this is my case to solve. The more you tell me, the quicker I can make that happen. We need to find the person who did this."

She grabbed at her hair and let it spill back around her face. "I don't know what to tell you. I've been back in Millbrook a couple of days. Tessa drove down today to spend the weekend with me. I was out running errands and checking on some of the homes I'm scheduled to furnish. When I got home, I called out her name and that's when…when he shot her and then he ran."

"What kind of errands? What kind of work?"

She gave him a look that should have been intimidating. It only made Blain more aware of her, in too many ways he shouldn't be aware. "I'm an interior designer. I work all over the Gulf Coast and all through Florida, decorating homes and condos, but lately in Tampa and down in Miami. I have a few clients up here, too."

"So you were with one of those clients?"

"I can provide a play-by-play of my afternoon, if you need me to, yes."

She was well-trained in deflecting questions, Blain decided. "And what about your sick mother?"

"I visited her before I went on my errands."

He wondered about the sick mother part, but Blain would get to the bottom of things, sooner or later. "Okay. So, I've got the timeline pretty much figured out. I'll have to wait to hear from the ME to find out the exact time of death. We've checked all of the upstairs rooms and according to my report, you told my officers that nothing important or valuable had been taken. But it looks like you might have surprised the intruder during a possible robbery."

He read over his notes again.

"But it could be that you returned home before the intruder could take anything valuable, which means we'll continue to comb the entire area around your home and see if we find any signs of someone getting away. We're questioning the neighbors and alerting the media, too. If there's a killer on the loose, everyone needs to be alert."

"I don't want the media hanging around," she blurted. Then she cast her gaze back toward the patio. "I… I need to absorb what just happened. Tessa never hurt anyone, never had an enemy. Everyone loved her." She whirled back to him. "I don't want the media to harass her family and friends."

Interesting. Or maybe she didn't want the media delving into her personal life?

He stopped and tried again. "We've collected

as much evidence as we can find for now so we'll take this up again first thing tomorrow, but there's still the matter of you finding another place to stay tonight."

She glared at him, sniffed back tears she seemed to be trying hard to ignore. "I'll go to a hotel."

"Okay, then," Blain said. "Get an overnight bag together and while you're up there in your bedroom, make sure you double-check everything. Things such as valuable jewelry that might be missing or maybe some cash you left in a purse."

She nodded. "Did you check the guest room? Tessa's room?"

Blain could tell she was slipping fast. She was going to crash soon so he needed to get her out of here. "Yes. Nothing out of the ordinary. Just your friend's purse with the contents dumped on the bed and some clothes scattered around. Everything still intact."

"Tessa is neat," she said, her gaze slamming into his. "She would have put her clothes away. She'd never leave her purse that way."

"Okay." He wrote that down.

"We were going out tonight," she said on a soft whisper. "Just for fun."

Blain remembered fun. "I'm sorry you have

to go through this," he said on a low note. "Do you want me to come upstairs with you?"

"No," she said. "I'll only be a few minutes."

"I'll be right here if you need anything."

He watched her up the stairs and then turned to take in the opulent design of the big town house. Did she decorate this one? Probably. A big pot with a healthy palm tree branching out around it sat by the ceiling-to-floor windows. A white leather couch and matching chair graced the spacious den. A modern-looking fireplace decorated in gold-and-white ornaments and shiny green foliage slashed across one wall and a bookshelf heavy with art and design books and a few novels filled the other wall. A vivid tropical-themed painting hung over the fireplace and a tall Christmas tree covered in silver-and-gold ornaments and ribbons stood in the corner by the fireplace.

So she'd been back in town long enough to get this place all gussied up for the holidays. Or maybe she'd hired someone to do it and they'd liked what they saw enough to try and rob the place. Maybe they'd sneaked inside the house, not knowing the other woman was here? Rikki had come home and surprised them? But why shoot the other woman?

Because she'd seen the intruder?

Now he had even more questions.

* * *

Rikki dreaded going into her bedroom. Knowing that a killer had gone through her house made her feel violated and ill at ease. She couldn't even look at the guest room where Tessa's things were scattered on the bed so she hurried up the hall to her room. She could see sparkling Christmas lights across the canal on another home's upper balcony. The lights were pretty but a chill rushed across her shoulders, making Rikki shake.

Tessa. Dead.

What a nightmare? Had she been wrong to come back here? No, she had to see her mother before it was too late. Before she had even more regrets to add to the long list already in her head.

And yes, she'd needed some time away from Chad Presley. Because Chad could never replace the one man she'd loved and lost, and once he'd realized that, he'd turned nasty.

But she wouldn't blame Chad. It wasn't his fault that she couldn't love him. Or that she'd never get over losing Drake.

Drake. Her sweet, young husband, Drake Allen.

We were so naive. So in love.

She missed him every day of her life but missing and wishing wouldn't bring him back. Rikki went about grabbing clothes and gathering the essentials, her mind so numb with shock she could barely walk.

She'd lost Drake years ago. And now she'd lost Tessa. And both had died violently. She'd never get beyond the shadow of her family's questionable legacy.

Staring at her pale reflection in the bathroom mirror, Rikki wondered how she'd ever be able to open her heart to anyone again. It was all too much.

Being back in Millbrook was too much.

And once her family heard about this, her nightmare would continue. Unless she left again. She could do that. Just run away and start over in another place all together.

You should tell Detective Kent the truth.

Maybe she should do that, level with him and get it all over with. But she didn't really know where to start. She didn't think Chad had it in him to follow her here and kill Tessa. In spite of his veiled threats, he was too busy making more money for himself. He didn't even know she'd left Tallahassee, anyway. Did he?

And her clients? While they all demanded discretion, none of them struck her as murderers. That left her powerful family. Could someone close to her actually want her dead?

No. Impossible. She'd been careful to stay out of trouble and to stay out of the limelight. None of this made sense. And like the detective, she wanted answers. Maybe they could work together on this if she leveled with him.

But right now, tonight, she didn't have the energy for a long confession. The handsome detective would find out about her soon enough, anyway. And then, she probably *would* become a suspect.

Blain checked his watch again. And again, he walked around the downstairs rooms of the town house.

The kitchen and dining room were open to the den, all white and bright, with more green plants and vivid artwork. A set of open stairs decorated with garland crawled up the wall by the entryway. Swanky, as his mom would say.

An officer came in while Blain moved around the room once again, anything to help him figure out who'd been through here. They'd already dusted for prints and searched for hair and fabric fibers but Blain doubted they'd find either. The place looked as pristine as one of the ads in his mother's many magazines. A professional job?

His gut burned toward that end but he still needed to pin her down on the ex-boyfriend. "What do you have, Wilson?" he asked the uniformed officer.

"Found some broken branches on the shrubbery near the back gate. The gate has a latch but no lock. Figure they left in a hurry headed that way once Miss Allen ran out screaming." He pointed toward a thicket of woods that followed the far shore of the river. "Anybody could get lost in there, even this time of year. We don't have a lot of bare trees in the winter around here."

"I hear that," Blain replied. A lot of pines and live oaks grew in that thicket. "Footprints? Shoe prints?"

"Yes, sir. Big ones. But only partials. A distinctive pattern, though."

"Get pictures and measurements. Maybe a plaster form."

"Already on it," Wilson replied. "I think we've covered everything for now."

"Okay. I'm waiting on Miss Allen," Blain said. "We're putting her in a hotel room for now. I'll need a cruiser to give us a ride and a guard on her room tonight."

The young officer nodded. "Night, Detective Kent."

Blain nodded and then checked his watch. What was keeping Rikki Allen? He was about to go up and check on her when she came back down with a fancy leather overnight bag on one arm and a smaller shoulder bag on the other shoulder.

"There you are," he said in what he hoped

was a casual voice. Taking her overnight bag, he said, "I thought you might have bolted on me."

She almost smiled. "I did consider it for about five minutes." The intense expression on her exotic face showed she'd considered it a lot.

"Why would you want to run away, Miss Allen?"

"Call me Rikki," she replied, not answering that question. "Now, can we get out of here?"

"Sure. I don't have my vehicle here so I'll have a patrol drop us at the hotel and I'll also assign a patrol outside your hotel."

"Did they break into Tessa's car? It should be in the public parking area around the corner."

"No. But we'll go over both your vehicles to see if we find any odd prints or maybe some fiber or hair follicles."

"What about you?" she asked, her head down. "How will you get back to your place?"

"I know my way home," he said, thinking he'd come right back here and do some more checking on his own.

Blain followed her to the front door where an officer was waiting to place crime-scene tape across the entryway and all around the small porch. Some of the neighbors were standing out on the boardwalk, their expressions full of shock and questions.

An officer walked them to a waiting patrol car.

Blain shot a glance toward the woman and remembered the sporty little convertible parked in her garage. Neither the car nor the woman would ever be his in this lifetime. Out of his league. So he needed to focus on work and not the subject at hand, his gut burning for answers.

She got in and glanced back after Blain put her stuff in the trunk and slid in beside her in the backseat. "I don't know what's going on. I don't know why someone would rob me and... kill Tessa."

"Are you sure you don't want to call your mother?" Maybe if he kept pushing, she'd keep talking.

"No. It's late and she's not well."

"I'm sorry to hear that. Who is your mother? I might know her."

"I doubt it."

Again, that nonresponse. "Okay."

Then she sat up on the seat. "What about Pebble?"

"Excuse me?"

"My cat, Pebble. He's missing."

"We'll put out some food for him and alert the neighbors."

The neighbors who were checking out their windows right about now and texting their friends and standing along the boardwalk in clusters of fear. Yeah, they'd definitely check with those neighbors.

He wouldn't push on that matter or the matter of her refusal to give him a straight answer, but he'd certainly do his own research later. So much for a slow holiday season.

He pulled out a business card when they approached the hotel she'd mentioned, one of the few low-budget hotels in town. At least this one was new and located near a busy intersection. No fancy condo-type accommodations around Millbrook. "Listen, if you need me for anything or if you remember anything, call me. No matter the time."

"I will."

Yeah, right.

He came around to help her out of the car but she already had her door open and herself out, tall boots and jean-clad legs first. He got the bag she'd packed out of the trunk. "I'll walk you to the front desk and make sure you're in a secure room."

"Okay."

Twenty minutes later, Blain was on his way to the station to file his report, his mind humming with the sure knowledge that Rikki Allen knew things she didn't want him to know. He'd head back to her town house once he was done with his work and look for her cat.

But he intended to find out the truth.

And while he did that, he'd try to get the image of those chocolate eyes and that matching hair out of his head. Blain's gut told him there was a lot more to Rikki Allen than she wanted anyone to know.

But he knew enough.

A beautiful, mysterious woman who'd broken up with her boyfriend and who'd obviously lived a life of privilege had interrupted an intruder in her home and had found her best friend dead. A best friend who resembled her. This case shouted hit man.

His job was to find out if someone wanted Rikki Allen dead. But he also wanted to figure out what she was trying so desperately to hide from the world.

THREE

Rikki tried to sleep but being alone in a strange room didn't help her to block out the image of Tessa, beautiful, sweet Tessa, lying there with blood all around her.

Tessa, who knew all of Rikki's secrets. A good friend—her college roommate—who'd taken Rikki under her wing after Drake had died and made her feel as if she wasn't going to lose her mind, after all.

Dear Lord, what happened to her? Help me understand. Help me to accept that she's in heaven with You now.

Blain had told her they'd notify Tessa's next of kin, but Tessa didn't have anyone close here in America since her parents had both passed away over recent years. Her one brother lived somewhere in Europe and Rikki didn't have any way to contact him. Tessa hadn't talked about her older brother a lot.

No one to mourn her. *Except me.*

Rikki had two big brothers, one married and one divorced, depending on which brother and which day, and several nieces and nephews, and a whole slew of aunts and uncles. A network of people who loved her in spite of how she'd abandoned all of them.

Santo and his family lived here and he ran the business now. He'd be all over her about this. Victor was somewhere in Europe. He'd turned his back completely on the family but he didn't mind using the family funds to party all over the world.

Rikki didn't want any of the mighty Alvanetti money.

She'd stayed long enough to appease her father and to reassure her mother, and then she'd left a few weeks after Drake's death. Forever, she'd thought. But she loved her mother and they'd kept in touch over the years. Sonia had always maintained that Drake's wreck was a tragedy. That no one has caused it.

Even so, when she got reports of her mother being taken ill while on a cruise overseas this summer, Rikki had kept in constant touch. But Sonia had not improved, and had had a heart attack as well, so she knew she had to come back. The doctors had verified that the vibrant Sonia Alvanetti had several other health complications and an onset of dementia, but with bed rest and a better diet and several prescriptions, she could improve. Maybe.

In other words, her mother could snap out of this or she could die in a few years. She could be giving up because she missed her one son who had left for good and she missed her daughter who kept promising to come and see her. Rikki's brother Victor didn't care that their mother had taken ill in Europe and he didn't care now. Rikki had come home to help her mother recover.

Rikki had been thinking of coming home since she'd noticed her mother didn't remember things and constantly repeated herself. Sometimes, she'd talk about her husband, the powerful Franco Alvanetti, as if she hated him. Which surprised Rikki. Her parents had always been so in love with each other that they oftentimes managed to shut out the rest of the world. Or ignore it, at least.

The kind of in-love that Rikki had given up on.

Rikki wished now that she'd come back sooner. But then, tonight she wished a lot of things could have been different.

She missed Tessa already. If she'd come home a few minutes earlier, she might have been able to save her friend.

This, with her mother so sick and her ex-boyfriend harassing her. It was just too much. Chad

Presley didn't like being dumped. He'd threatened Rikki one time too many and he had powerful friends all over the state. But then, so did her father.

And using that angle had been her saving grace.

"If you don't leave me alone, Chad, I'll have to tell my father and my brothers. You won't like it when they come after you."

The bluff had worked long enough for her to regroup and come home. But maybe Chad wasn't afraid of her family. She should have told the detective the whole story but fear had gripped her, choking her with an intense power. Fear that Chad would make good on his promises and fear that her family would get involved if he did.

A chill moved through her at the thought of Chad finding her here. Would he think to send someone to spy on her? Or had he followed through on one of his threats and found her himself?

Maybe he'd killed Tessa to prove a point. He'd stalked Rikki time and time again but things had never become physical. What if he'd thought he'd found *her* there on the patio? Chad could be the kind to shoot first and run away like a coward.

Please, no.

Rikki called the night nurse at her parents'

estate, just to hear someone's voice and to check on her mom. "How's she doing tonight, Peggy?"

"Sleeping, suga'. But you know Miss Sonia. She has the sweetest attitude."

"Yes, that's Mother. Always positive. Even when she's in pain."

"I've got her all tucked in and I'll be right here on the sofa in her bedroom."

"Thank you, Peggy." Rikki swallowed the emotion roiling through her. "What about Papa?"

"He's in his office. He stays in there, most days."

Rikki closed her eyes to that image. Her dad was getting old, too. "I'll try to check on him."

"You gonna come by in the morning, honey?"

"I hope to." Rikki didn't want her mother to hear anything about what had happened, but Peggy kept the television off most of the time, anyway. She liked to read her romance novels while the surround sound played Mother's favorite classical music and show tunes. A paradox of a combination but that was Sonia Alvanetti.

But her father always watched the local news. She'd have to explain this to him so he wouldn't get involved. Of course, one of his bodyguards had probably already informed him of what had happened. His people kept their ears to the ground.

"Give her a kiss for me," Rikki said. "I'll be

by bright and early tomorrow morning." And she'd try to explain things to her mother. Of course, once her brothers got wind of this…

Rikki put that scene out of her mind. Her two brothers would hunt down anyone who tried to harm her. Even when they both disapproved of her every move.

"I'll see you before you turn things over to the day nurse," she promised Peggy.

"Okay, sweetie pie." Peggy said good-night and Rikki went back to the dark silence of her room.

Thinking about the horror of seeing her best friend dead, Rikki closed her eyes but opened them wide again, the shadows of the spacious room chasing each other into dark corners. She checked the door. Locked and bolted. She looked at the heavy curtains. Closed tight. She listened for footsteps and remembered a cruiser was supposed to be parked outside her hotel room door. But each shift of the wind caused her to panic and recheck the locked door.

Then because she couldn't sleep, she thought about Detective Blain Kent. Tall, dark and dangerous. But on the good side of the law. Well, that was different at least. The man knew his job, no doubt about that. He'd done his best to get information out of Rikki and she'd given him what he needed and kept the rest to herself.

While her heart hurt for her friend and she'd mourn that loss of the rest of her life, Rikki took comfort in knowing if anyone could figure this out Blain Kent would be the man. He struck her as the honest, determined type.

And what if he figures out who you are?

At this point, she didn't really care if the detective with the midnight-blue eyes and clipped black hair found out she was an Alvanetti. She had been married once, to Drake Allen. A good, simple name and a good simple man. No, a boy, really. A boy who'd loved her in spite of her name. He'd been willing to fight for her and that had been a tragic mistake.

He'd died too young and her heart had not recovered.

He'd died at the hands of her family, something she could never prove. Something they'd denied. But she knew. Drake had been in a horrible accident not too far from the Alvanetti estate. A foggy night, a slick road. And alcohol. But Drake didn't drink.

No one had wanted to hear her shouting that at the top of her lungs. No one cared enough to investigate. And she surely would never recover from that, either.

But once she'd been strong enough to come up with a plan, she'd walked away from her father's rules as soon as she could escape. Walked away and tried to stay away. Except her beautiful, stubborn, scatterbrained mother always called her back. Sonia Alvanetti had a heart so big Rikki wondered how she'd become so frail. Had often wondered how her sweet mother could not see the truth regarding the family "import-export" business. Rikki had always believed her mother would live forever since Sonia loved everyone in such an unconditional way. She couldn't imagine her mother not being there. Rikki had got her strong faith from her mother, thankfully.

That faith would get her through this long night.

Now Rikki had to wonder about what Blain Kent had pointed out to her earlier. She and Tessa did look a lot alike.

Which made Rikki wonder if her worst fears and the detective's not-so-subtle hints were correct. Had that bullet been meant for her?

Blain's phone buzzed a rude alert. He sat up in bed and watched his phone dancing across the nightstand. Then he jerked it to his ear. "Kent."

"I… I need your help again."

"Rikki?"

"Yes."

She sounded muffled, scared.

Blain shot out of the bed and started grabbing

clothes with one hand, the cell phone tucked between his ear and his collar bone. "What is it?"

"Someone came to my room."

Blain's pulse bumped into overdrive. "Are you still in the room?"

"No. I shouted that I was calling 911 and then I started screaming and banging on the walls. Then I called the front desk. The security guard apparently came out and scared away the intruder. I don't know where the patrol officer is."

Blain hopped on one foot trying to get his boots on. "Okay, where are you now?"

"In the lobby bathroom. I didn't know who else to call."

"I'll be there in five minutes. Do not leave the hotel lobby area."

"I won't."

"Stay on the phone with me," Blain said. "I'm leaving right now." He glanced around and saw Pebble the cat staring at him from the end of his bed. He'd found the cat by the back door of her place, meowing and scared. The mostly black-and-white long-haired calico did look like a pile of pebbles.

So now he had custody of a cat. He'd worry about Pebble later. He hurried out the door of his apartment and hoped Rikki Alvanetti would stay put until he could get to her.

She did as he asked and by the time Blain

made it to the hotel, he'd gotten more information out of her. She'd been awake, unable to sleep, when she'd heard someone outside her door. Then the door handle had jiggled. She'd screamed out and threatened to call 911.

But she'd called him instead. Blain radioed in while he kept her on the phone. When he pulled up, two units were parked in the drive-through in front of the bright lobby. But he didn't see the other cruiser or Rikki, either.

"I'm here," he said into his cell. "Come out of the bathroom, Rikki."

"Okay."

He ended the call, furious that someone had tried to get to her in spite of their efforts. But this attack supported his suspicions. Someone was after Rikki Allen.

"Where's our man?" he asked one of the uniformed officers as he slammed out of his unmarked sedan.

"He *was* knocked out in the bushes but on his way to the ER right now," one of the patrolmen said. "He'll be okay."

The man they'd put on Rikki had gotten out of his patrol car to stretch his legs and chat with the pretty front-desk clerk. When he'd returned to his car, he'd been hit on the head and knocked out. Another officer had taken him to the hospital in his patrol car.

Sometimes, small-town police officers did things in a backward kind of way but Blain knew his fellow officers were all hardworking men. He was just glad everyone was okay.

Especially the woman emerging pale and sleep-tousled out of the bathroom. She looked at Blain and walked straight toward him, wearing a dark red zipped jacket and matching pants that his mother would call lounge wear.

He called it nice-looking wear right now but he kept his mind focused on the task and not the way that combo fit Rikki. "Hey, you okay?"

"Yes." She glanced around, not looking so okay. "Did you find anyone out there?"

"Not yet. My men are searching every nook. We'll double-check the area around your door, but I'm guessing whoever found you knew to wear gloves and not leave any clues."

She nodded and pushed at all that tumbling hair. "Now we know, Detective."

"Know what?" He didn't like the gleam of acceptance in her eyes.

"That they were after me."

"Yes, I believe you're right on that," Blain replied. "But they could have been after both of you." At the look of horror on her face, he said, "Listen, you're gonna have to tell me where your mother lives. You can't stay here alone."

"I can't have them in her house, either."

"But you'll be with someone and… I'll make sure no one bothers either of you."

"And what are you, a one-man type of super-hero?"

"No, but I think I can patrol a home and keep intruders out."

"He's a former marine, ma'am," a passing officer said in a matter-of-fact tone. "He can take care of you."

She quirked a dark eyebrow and took a calming breath. "A marine? So that should make me feel safe, I suppose."

"One of the best," the young patrolman said before Blain could reply. "An MP at that. Only, he don't like to brag."

Blain shook his head. "Look, I can watch over you tonight."

She stared at him with a new regard, her dark gaze sweeping over him and making him squirm. "I don't want to go to my mother's house."

Blain took her by the arm and tugged her off to the side where no one could hear him. "Your place isn't safe. This hotel isn't safe even though we had a uniformed patrol on site. I can't take you to my place. Unless you have somewhere you can go that you can assure me is okay, then you'd better tell me the truth, Miss Allen. All of it. Or I'll have to take you to the station and put you in a cell just to make sure you *are* safe until morning."

"I don't know the truth," she said, her voice weakening. "I've told you everything I can." Then she shook her head. "I keep thinking of Chad—my ex. But he couldn't be this stupid. He's threatened me but… I can't believe he'd do this. He has too much at stake."

Blain held his lips tightly together to keep from shouting at her. "And it never occurred to you to give me these details when you mentioned him earlier?"

"I didn't think he'd find me at the town house. I never told him that my family—that I own it."

"Well, maybe he followed you and…tried to kill you." Blain pulled out his notebook. "What's his address?"

She hesitated and then gave him Chad's workplace and home addresses.

"And when did you last see Chad Presley?"

"About a week ago, down in Miami."

Blain got a description of Chad and his vehicle and put out a BOLO over the radio that would go statewide. Be On the Lookout for a possible killer.

"There. We'll see what that turns up. Does this Chad know where your mother lives?"

She thought about last spring when she'd

brought him here for a wedding. That hadn't gone over very well.

"He's been here before but only once."

"Okay, then, let's go. Either you tell me where to take you or…you can spend the night in jail."

"You can't do that—force me into jail."

"I can if it's for your own good."

He didn't like playing bad cop with her, but the woman was too stubborn to see that someone was after her. And a nasty ex-boyfriend would be a prime suspect. Surely she wasn't one of those women who kept forgiving over and over until it was too late.

Blain would find out everything about her before this was over, but right now he wanted to get her out of here. They were too exposed at this location now.

She finally nodded. "I need to get my things."

After he escorted her to her room, he put her in his car and turned to stare at her. "Where to, princess?"

She swallowed, dropped her head and stared at her hands in her lap. "The Bay Road."

Bay Road? Blain whistled. Real estate out there was way over his pay-scale. "Okay, then."

Pricey estates out there. A scenic highway surrounding where the big bay met up with Millbrook Lake.

When they were underway and out past the

city, he turned off and followed the dark water. "Which address?"

She finally looked over at him, a solid defiance in her voice. "2200 First Bay Lane."

Blain blinked, thinking he hadn't heard right. "Hey, that's—"

"The Alvanetti estate," she finished for him. "Sonia Alvanetti is my mother."

Blain held tightly to the steering wheel as realization settled around him. "And… Franco Alvanetti is your father."

"Yes." She nodded and looked out the window.

And suddenly, Blain understood so much more about what was going on with Rikki Allen. No wonder she'd been so closemouthed and evasive. No wonder he couldn't trust her.

She was an Alvanetti.

FOUR

Old Florida.

A wrought-iron gate swung open after Rikki gave him a security code to punch in on the big electronic switch pad.

Blain eased the unmarked police sedan along the winding lane and took in his surroundings as the first rays of the sun shone like a spotlight through the trees.

Swaying palm trees and palmetto bushes, massive live oaks dripping with Spanish moss. Scattered orange and lemon trees that would be lush with fruit come next summer. Winter-white camellias blooming on deeply rooted bushes. Wild magnolia trees shooting up through the oaks, their fat, waxy leaves hanging heavy and dark green along the winding garden paths on either side of the private gravel-and-shell-covered drive.

And what looked like a big white barn and

stables surrounded by a white board fence off in the distance.

The wild abandonment of this tropical landscape didn't fool Blain. This kind of exotic display spoke of money as old as the camellia bushes. Dirty money.

The sparkling sunrise brought the light of dawn peeking through the heavy foliage like a diamond hidden in the forest. And then, the stark stucco mansion came into view, all creamy planes and angles and glass against rich brown teakwood trim aged with a shimmering patina that shone in the early morning light.

Blain pulled the sedan up to the six-car garage and turned off the engine. Still in shock, he pivoted in his seat toward Rikki. "Why did you lie to me?"

"I didn't lie," she said, her gaze slamming him with an unapologetic attitude. "I… I don't associate with my family very much since I left. I only keep in touch with my mother."

"You could have told me that." He studied the house. "Or at least who your mother really is."

"And you would have immediately jumped to the wrong conclusion."

She was correct there. He would have jumped to the only conclusion and it wasn't a good one. "I want the truth," he snapped. "Now I doubt I'll ever get it from you."

"I gave you the truth," she retorted. "I told you everything I knew, even about my ex-boyfriend. I was so afraid he'd done this I couldn't bring myself to mention him at first. But I should have. If it's him, I have to get out of here." She took a deep, shuddering breath. "I don't know. Could he be the one? I can't let him get away with killing my best friend."

Blain could see the fear and concern in her dark eyes. He understood how abused women could spin a situation to justify why they always returned but he couldn't understand why she hadn't leveled with him to begin with since her best friend *had* been murdered. There was no returning to that.

He'd have to think this one through but right now, he had to make sure Rikki was safe. Keeping her alive meant he had to deal with the entire situation, whether he liked it or not.

Blain lifted his hand in the air. "He can't hurt anyone inside the gates to this compound. I saw the cameras and I spotted an armed guard with a dog, too."

"Yes," she said, nodding. "If Chad shows up here, they'll probably kill him and then I'll have that death on my hands, too."

Blain grabbed her wrist. "What do you mean, too? Do you think your *family* killed Tessa?"

"No." She gave him an imploring stare. "I was

married once when I was around twenty. His last name was Allen. Drake Allen. But he died six months after we eloped."

Blain let that tidbit of information sink in. That explained the last name she used. "How did he die?"

"An accident." Lowering her head, she added, "Up on the road."

"But you think your family took care of him?"

"I didn't say that." She opened the door and got out of the car, her attitude like a solid wall against him. She might have cut all ties to her powerful family, but blood always ran thicker than water. She wouldn't rat anybody out.

Blain got out of the car and came around to meet her, some of his justified anger simmering into a slow boil. She didn't have to say what had happened to her husband. He could see it all over her face. "So you blame yourself?"

"Yes." She whirled and opened the back car door to get her stuff. "But my mother is innocent. She thinks Drake died in a car crash and he did. I've never been able to prove otherwise."

Shoving one of the bags at him, she said, "So if you insist on going inside with me, you'd better keep quiet about what I just told you. As far as I know, over the last few years, my father has changed. He's not the same man he used to be. He's legitimate now."

"Yeah, because he's turned things over to your brothers."

"I can't speak to that since I don't keep up with them. One is here, running the business and the other one in Europe. I told you I walked away a long time ago. I only came here to get away from Chad for a while and to be with my mother." She stared up at the massive glass doors of the house where two evergreen wreaths hung side by side. "It is Christmas, after all."

Blain couldn't force her to tell him everything. Not yet, anyway. But now that he knew who she really was, things had taken on a whole new meaning. "I'll get you safely inside to see your mother, but I strongly suggest you stay here. Don't go anywhere, understand? I have to do some digging on Chad Presley and I want to go back over the details of your friend's death. That means I might be back to ask you some more questions."

"I'll be right here," she said. "I do have a few clients to meet with this week but I can do video conferences for now and change those appointments to later."

"Much later," Blain retorted. "Like after we find out who killed Tessa."

"Then you'd better get to it." She hurried toward the portico door on the side of the big house near the garage. Turning, she gave him a conflicted stare. "I'm not like them, Blain. I got away and created my own life, on my own terms."

Blain saw the defiant expression behind that sincere statement. Maybe he should cut her some slack. But he wouldn't do her any favors. He refused to look the other way like his dad had done all those years. "I sure hope that's true. I'll have someone bring your car out here once I think it's safe to move it. Remember, don't go anywhere for the next few days."

She nodded, one hand on the brass door handle. "Thank you." Then she glanced around and back into his eyes. "I appreciate all your help."

"Doing my job," he said. Then he took his time scoping the entire place before he got in his car and left.

Rikki entered the side door that opened into the butler's pantry leading to the massive gourmet kitchen where her mother used to cook and entertain on a weekly basis. Those days were few and far between now that her mother had gotten sick. Her parents were probably lonely, but no one wanted to acknowledge that. Nor did anyone want to admit that soon they wouldn't be able to live here alone. They both had failing health these days, according to Peggy's reports to Rikki.

The last big event held here had been Rikki's cousin Beatrice's wedding back in the spring. Rikki had come home for the wedding but she'd gotten here a few minutes before the ceremony and even though her mother had begged her to stay, she'd left about thirty minutes into the reception. She and Chad had been fighting. Again.

That had been the last time she'd seen her mother happy and laughing. Sonia had always loved having people in her home. Her mother had left that afternoon for a European vacation.

A few days later, Rikki had received a call that her mother had taken ill while on a Mediterranean cruise and was sent to a hospital in Italy where her brother Victor was staying at the time. Rikki had gone over to see her mother, but Victor had already left the hospital. He obviously was too busy to even sit with his mother.

Rikki had stayed there until her mother was able to make the flight home to Florida, where Franco had met her with a private ambulance and an equally private nurse.

Now Rikki took her time walking through the long, spacious kitchen with the dark cabinets and the white marble countertops. The kitchen opened to a big dining area and a spacious den, complete with a fire in the enormous fireplace and comfy leather sofas and chairs scattered all around. High, wide windows looked out over a prime spot where Millbrook Lake met up with the big bay that would take boaters all the way out to the Gulf.

Rikki glanced out at the sloping yard down to the lake where a boathouse and her father's yacht—the *Sonia*—sat moored to the big private dock. The pool glistened in the early morning light, the sun hitting the water with a brilliant clarity that Rikki could only pray she had. When she heard footsteps shuffling up the long central hallway that led to her mother and father's private suite in the back of the house, she whirled, expecting to see Peggy. The always-positive redhaired nurse had been with her mother since Sonia had come home a few months ago. But Peggy had worked for her family for as long as Rikki could remember, helping to raise children and take care of sick relatives.

Her mother adored Peggy and Peggy adored her mother.

But Peggy wasn't standing there in the archway near the stairs to the second floor. Franco Alvanetti stopped to stare at his only daughter. "Well, I see you have arrived, at last."

Rikki hated the tremble inside her heart. "Yes, Father. I got here yesterday but—"

"But you had to give the locals a report on the woman they found shot to death on your townhome patio."

His bloodshot eyes moved over her with a steady gaze that left most people quaking. Rikki had long ago learned to stop the quaking but she had to take a few calming breaths to make it work today. "So you know."

"Of course I know," he said as he moved toward her in a stooped, aged gait. "I still have friends around this town."

Her father wore a plaid robe over old silk pajamas. His slippers were Italian leather, worn in spots but still expensive-looking. Even in his night clothes with his salt-and-pepper hair scattered around his olive-skinned face, he still commanded a certain respect.

Rikki reluctantly gave him that respect. "I didn't want to upset Mother."

"She is sleeping. Peggy will be out soon to give the morning report."

He glanced toward the kitchen. "Coffee, Regina?"

"Yes, Papa, but I'll make it."

"Good." He waved a hand toward the industrial-sized coffee machine. "And then we can sit down and talk about this latest scandal in your life."

Rikki went to the cabinet and found the coffee, steeling herself against one of Franco's soft-spoken interrogations. They used to have several servants in the house but lately, it was just her parents and a maid who cleaned and cooked, along with a day nurse. Her parents didn't require much in the way of food or drink. Peggy and the day nurse made sure they both had nutritious food to eat.

When had her parents become so frail?

Feeling guilty for not checking on them more, Rikki blinked away her tears and her fatigue. "Would you like some breakfast, Papa?"

Her father glanced up from where he'd perched on a bar stool in the way he'd done on countless mornings. "You know, I miss your mother's cooking. She used to make the best omelets."

Rikki closed her eyes, the smell of breakfast wafting out as if her mother were standing at the big stove cooking and laughing and talking about her plans for the day. Sonia always had her days planned out for months, down to the pumps and jewelry she'd wear that day.

"Of course, I'll make you an omelet," Rikki said. Once she had the coffee brewing, Rikki pulled out eggs, cream, cheese and vegetables.

"Throw in some bacon," her father said.

When she nodded and glanced back at him, he had his head in his hands, his face down. His once-dark hair was salt-and-pepper now and his always-meaty hands were puffy with excess fluid. She'd noticed the deep bags underneath his eyes, too. Had he stopped taking care of himself?

Rikki turned back to her work, wishing she could say something to him but then she'd never understood her brooding, distant father. Only Sonia could bring out his jovial, loving side. Her mother shone like a star in all of their lives and Sonia's strong faith held them all together.

"I'll pray you through it," her mother always said, no matter what they were dealing with. "God has blessed us in spite of it all. He'll continue to bless us."

I'll pray you through it.

Maybe it was Rikki's turn to pray them through the latest tragedy, to pray for Blain and the local police, to pray for Tessa's brother who didn't even know she was dead yet. And to pray for herself and her family, no matter what.

But right now, she'd cook for her father. For a few minutes, she could forget about her rift with this man, forget about her mother's illness and her own failures in life, and maybe for just this little while, she could forget about Tessa's vacant, lifeless eyes staring up at her from a pool of blood.

Maybe she could even forget about the way Blain Kent's expression had changed when he'd realized who she really was, too. Because she knew the good-looking detective would hound her until he figured out what kind of trouble she'd brought back to Millbrook with her.

Rikki intended to find out the answer to that question herself, with or without Blain's help.

Putting all of that aside, she flipped the omelet onto a plate and brought it over to her father with a steaming cup of black coffee. "Here you go, Papa."

Franco Alvanetti looked up at her with misty eyes. "This is a good moment," he said. "Too bad about your friend."

Rikki couldn't decide if her father was being sincere or not, but she felt that trembling in her heart again.

Was it raw emotion? Or was it a warning to be aware?

FIVE

Blain sat at his desk in the back corner of the Millbrook Police Department, scrolling through some old news articles about the Alvanetti family. He'd read up on their philanthropic endeavors, their weddings, births, deaths and celebrations plus a few articles questioning certain tactics they used in their so-called import-export business located in a huge warehouse just outside of town.

But nothing much on their only daughter's brief marriage to Drake Allen. Nothing much about his fatal car crash but the accident report told the tale. High rate of speed and alcohol.

End of report. Could it be possible that Rikki just needed someone to blame so her grief wouldn't cut so deep?

"Kent, what've you got on the Tessa Jones case?"

Blain glanced up to find his chubby, mustached police chief, Raymond Ferrier, staring down at him like a curious bulldog. The chief trusted Blain but he was antsy about this high-profile murder, especially now that he knew it had happened at a place owned by an Alvanetti.

"Not much, sir." That was true. He hadn't found a whole lot on the Jones woman. "She lived in Tallahassee so I've got a couple of detectives there casing out friends and family. I had one of my contacts there who's tracking down the boyfriend. He's supposed to get back to me after he talks to the boyfriend and finds out where he was yesterday."

"Not good, right here at the holidays," the chief said. "I feel for Miss Alvanetti but I can't have a bunch of nervous-Nellie citizens suggesting we call off the Christmas parade or cancel the cantata at Millbrook Lake Church because they think a killer is on the loose."

"Not gonna let that happen, Chief," Blain replied, wishing the chief would quit breathing down his neck so he could get back to work. "I'm researching articles right now, trying to put things together." He shuffled through the report. "Besides, I don't think anything can get in the way of the Christmas parade."

Chief Ferrier shook his head, the red lines along his neck turning crimson. "Just keep at it. I sure don't need Old Man Alvanetti demanding justice. We all know how that'll turn out."

"I'll handle that," Blain replied. The chief had never caved underneath the Alvanetti juggernaut but he wasn't too thrilled to have to stand in the way of that juggernaut either. Up until now, things had been pretty quiet on that front. "I'm going back out to the house to question Regina Alvanetti later today."

The chief scrubbed a hand down his always-a-day-behind-beard stubble. "Be careful about that. You know how things tend to go out at that place."

"I'm always careful," Blain said. And he wasn't afraid of the Alvanetti clan. Rikki owed him and he intended to cash in on that debt. Plus, he had one furry, demanding cat to deliver.

Chief Ferrier grunted at that confident retort. "Careful is one thing, son. But being smart is important, too."

After the chief went back to his office, Blain jotted a list of all the variables on this case. The victim resembled Regina—Rikki—Alvanetti. They'd been best friends. Rikki had a hostile ex-boyfriend named Chad Presley but he hadn't been located yet. The Tallahassee authorities called to let Blain know they had talked to Tessa Jones's boyfriend and his alibi was solid. That left Chad Presley.

Nothing of importance had been taken from the town house and there was no sign of forced entry. Blain decided this was looking more like a professional hit than a crime of passion.

Had Tessa known her murderer? What did the "K" written in blood mean? Was it an initial or had the poor woman just been grasping at the floor, trying to get up? He'd have to wait for the ballistics report and lab work to come back on the autopsy from the state lab in Tallahassee. But while he waited, Blain intended to keep plugging away, trying to find the truth.

He thought about Rikki Alvanetti. Lush and exotic, much in the same way as that imposing home and the dubious lifestyle she had tried so hard to deny. She had grown up privileged and entitled in a world that most plain folks only dreamed about.

That was about to change. Blain wouldn't let her big brown eyes or her tragic demeanor fool him. He'd ignore the tickle of awareness her spice-scented perfume caused in his system and he'd certainly ignore those black boots she wore with such an easy, classy sway.

Blain could be tenacious when he was on a case and this one was a doozy. He'd already had calls from several television stations and most of the local and regional papers, all wanting to interview him regarding the Tessa Jones murder—and how it might be connected to the mighty Alvanetti family.

"No comment."

He couldn't talk about an active case. He'd let the people in the mayor's PR department give out the talking points. He'd rather get out and beat the bushes to find out the truth.

He had to wonder if Rikki knew more than she was telling him. His trust meter on her had gone down, way down, when she'd taken him to the Alvanetti estate. Even more when he'd realized she was one of them.

He was about to head out there to confront her one more time when his cell rang.

Preacher.

"Hey," he said into the phone as he grabbed his leather jacket and walked toward the front door of the small police building right across from the county courthouse. "What's happening, Preacher?"

Rory Sanderson's laugh rolled out on a low wave. "You tell me. I'm thinking you're up to your eyeballs on this murder that happened last night."

"You got that right," Blain said. He stopped in the parking lot, near his car. "I guess I'll be the hot topic at pizza night, right?"

Blain and his three buddies always met once a week for pizza and watching sports on the popular Back Bay Pizza House.

"We're all waiting for Thursday at seven

o'clock to come," Rory replied. "I just called to tell you if things get crazy—"

"You will pray for me, right?"

"Oh, I do that, anyway," the always cheerful minister replied. "I mean, if this case gets as in-depth as I think it will, you'll need someone to listen to your rants."

"I know you got my back," Blain said, thanking God for his friends.

Rory Sanderson was the popular and much-loved minister at Millbrook Lake Church now, but he'd been a chaplain in the army just a few years ago. Another member of their group was Alec Caldwell, a former marine who'd been injured and had the scars to prove it, and was now a successful businessman living in one of the old Victorian houses along the lake. Even though he'd inherited a ton of money from his late mother, he was as laid-back and unassuming as any man could be since he'd met local bakery owner Marla Hamilton. They were getting married in two weeks and Blain was the best man.

Rory would officiate and who knew what their fourth man, Hunter Lawson, would do or if he'd even show up for the wedding. The Okie came and went like a shadow but he was slowly growing on all of them and he was a solid friend if need be. Blain might have to call Hunter since

Hunter had gotten his PI license recently and was now available to work cases in the state of Florida.

"So I know you can't talk about the case but... be careful out there," Rory said. "This is a bit off the reservation for Millbrook."

"Yeah, and don't I know it," Blain replied. "I'll be careful. And smart."

"I'll see you soon," Rory said.

Blain hit End and turned to unlock his car. Then he noticed he had a flat tire. "What?"

He bent to examine the tire. He'd just had the vehicle serviced, courtesy of the Millbrook Police Department since it was a departmental vehicle. The mechanics had suggested new tires so he'd had those put on, too.

Now this. Blain studied the tire and noticed something odd. A slash mark cutting deep into the still-new tread.

Suddenly, he wasn't as worried about how the department's money had gone to waste on these tires as he was about how someone had obviously slashed this tire in broad daylight.

Blain heaved an aggravated sigh and stood up to check his surroundings, thinking he'd just gotten his first hint on how things would go with an investigation involving an Alvanetti.

Or maybe, his first warning from a killer.

* * *

Rikki sat holding her mother's frail hand.

Sonia was sleeping, which was a surprise in itself. Her mother used to rise with the dawn because she had to see the sun cresting out over the water to the east. She'd make herself a strong cup of coffee and stroll down to the dock so she could be as close to the water as possible to watch the sunrise.

"Isn't that amazing?" she'd say to anyone who might want to venture down with her at the crack of dawn. "God's world is so full of joy and beauty. That same sun that shines on us each day covers the entire earth with warmth. That sun shines on all of us, Rikki. You always remember that, no matter where you are in life. Always look toward the sun, honey."

Rikki brushed at the tears in her eyes and glanced at the clock. It was midmorning but the heavy curtains in her parents' bedroom were still drawn shut.

"Hey, Mama, want me to open the curtains so you can see the sunshine?"

Sonia let out a little grunt but didn't wake up.

Franco had left for the day with the excuse that he needed to visit with Santo at the warehouse and go over some paperwork.

Rikki probably should let her mother sleep

but Peggy had suggested trying to wake her in hopes that seeing Rikki would help Sonia. "She needs to get her strength back but she has a hard time staying up. Mr. A tries to get her to take a walk with him out to the water, but she just can't make it."

Rikki wanted her mother to make it. Determined and needing something positive to cling to after the last couple of days, Rikki went to the row of glass windows and opened the curtains to the big sliding doors that were usually flung open to the back garden. While the water looked inviting, the chilly temperature forced the doors to stay shut tight.

At least a cozy fire burned in the bedroom fireplace and Peggy had put up a glittering gold-and-red ornamented Christmas tree between the two high-backed brocade chairs in the corner by the doors. If she could get her mother to make it to a chair...

A knock at the bedroom door pulled Rikki out of her hopes.

The day nurse, Daphne, leaned her head in, her short brown curls falling in her eyes. "You have a visitor, Miss Alvanetti. Blain Kent."

Rikki's heart jumped so fast she had to catch her breath. Whirling, she left the drapery gaping open. "I'll be right there. Thank you, Daphne."

The pretty young nurse nodded and went back

to the kitchen where she was making soup that no one would probably eat.

"I'll be back soon, Mama," Rikki whispered. She kissed her mother's soft cheek and brushed back the spiky white-blond hair Sonia had always been so proud of.

Sonia mumbled incoherently but kept sleeping.

Rikki stopped in the wide hallway and gathered herself. Her mother used to say, "Pull yourself together and put on some color."

Rikki checked her light pink lipstick and ran a hand through her tousled hair out of habit, thinking of her mother's endearing command. Just one of many Sonia quoted often. Then she took her time making her way to the far side of the long house.

Blain was waiting in the den. He stood in front of the fire, staring at the family portrait centered over the mantel.

Daphne was still in the kitchen. She sent Rikki an inquisitive glance and then gazed back across the way at Blain.

Rikki's heart jumped again. He was an attractive man. All hard angles and dark shaggy hair, his physique muscular and solid. He wore a worn black leather jacket and jeans with battered cowboy boots.

"Detective," she said by way of a greeting. "You're out early today."

At the sound of her flats hitting the hardwood floors, he turned and swept her with a questioning gaze. And he was holding her squirming cat.

Something melted inside Rikki's bitter heart. But she poured all that softness into grabbing Pebble up in her arms and cooing to him. "You found him. Thank you."

Blain gave her an indulgent stare and wiped cat hair off his jacket. "He found me outside your town house. And now I have cat hair all over my apartment." He pointed to the bag of dry cat food on the counter. "Got this at the discount store."

"Thank you." She smiled at his obvious disapproval. "Pebble is an early riser. I'm sure he woke you to let you know he needed feeding."

"I've been up for a while," he retorted. "How'd you sleep last night?"

The question rang out more as an accusation. "Better than the night before," she replied, determined not to give him any openings.

She dropped Pebble and watched as the big cat ran to the kitchen and meowed. She moved across the room to find a bowl, and motioned toward the big leather sectional. "Have a seat. Can I get you some coffee?"

He sniffed toward the kitchen. "I thought I

smelled actual real coffee. That stuff we have at the station is more like tar mixed with motor oil."

"I'll bring you a cup right away. Cream and sugar?"

He gave her a look that spoke of something besides coffee. "No. Black. Thank you."

Rikki headed toward the kitchen where Daphne was bent down petting Pebble and smiled at the curious nurse. "Daphne, would you mind sitting with my mother while I talk to the detective?"

Daphne nodded, pursed her lips, turned off the stove and then left the room. Too nosy, that one. Or maybe too interested in the brooding man sitting in the den.

"Here you go." After feeding the cat, Rikki came back to the den and handed Blain the big Christmas mug, one of many her mother had collected over the years. This one had a grinning reindeer on it.

Blain stared at the silly mug, one dark eyebrow lifting. With a smile so quick it could have been a wink, he took the coffee and drank deeply. "Good. Very good."

If she hadn't been so unsettled by seeing him, Rikki would have laughed. "I'm glad you approve."

He sat down and turned to business, his whole

demeanor turning as black as the coffee. "I need to ask you a few more questions."

Rikki sank down on the other side of the sectional. "Of course." She swallowed and tried to calm herself."

She willed herself not to break down in front of him. She'd cried enough yesterday and last night, seeing her mother so frail and knowing she'd never see Tessa alive again. "Okay. Well, I'd like to help with her funerals expenses whenever that's possible. I owe her family a lot."

"Why's that?"

Did he have to distrust everything she said?

"When I first left Millbrook, they took me in and let me stay with them until Tessa and I could go to FSU together. She was my roommate all the way through college." She stared out at the water beyond the yard. "Her mother died of lung cancer when Tessa and I were in college and her father died later in a boating accident. I miss them and now I'll miss her."

"So you two were close."

"Yes. I told you she was my best friend. I don't know what I'll do without her."

Blain lowered his gaze and took a sip of coffee, but Rikki thought she'd seen a trace of compassion passing through his inky eyes. Gone in a flash but something to remember when he started grilling her.

He studied his notes then glanced back up at her. "Okay, so, your ex might have an alibi. We haven't located him yet, but several neighbors saw him at a company Christmas party the night of the murder. We checked with his coworkers and several of them vouched for his whereabouts yesterday."

Rikki nodded. "Probably at that party with his new girlfriend."

"So he still stalks you while he's dating another woman?"

She colored with humiliation. "I tend to attract real losers. He dated other people while we were together, too."

He gave her another in-depth sweeping gaze that didn't seem to have anything to do with the conversation. Almost like a silent compliment.

"So…your Charming Chad was in Tallahassee with a roomful of people at the time of the murder. We have pictures and we have statements that both support his statement. He's in the clear for now since the ME established the time of death at around 6:00 p.m."

"So you can mark him off your suspect list?"

"Yes. For now." He studied his notes. "But he didn't show up for work today. We're still trying to locate him."

A thread of apprehension curled down her spine. "That's odd. Chad never misses work."

"We'll keep checking. He might have a hang-over or maybe he took a day off." The detective didn't look too concerned. "Now on to you."

Rikki knew this man still had his doubts about her. "And what about me, Detective? What list am I on?"

SIX

Blain wasn't sure how to answer that question. He leaned forward and cupped his hands together. "I'd like to believe you're on the good list but I haven't talked to Santa yet."

Her smile wasn't as confident as she probably hoped it would be. "Don't do me any favors."

"Hadn't planned on it," he retorted, thinking he'd have to go to the extreme to make that a true statement. "But I still need to ask you a few more questions."

Rikki sat back on her side of the couch, her hands clasped. "I'll tell you anything you want to know. Just please find Tessa's killer."

Blain intended to do just that. "Tessa's boyfriend's alibi held. He had several witnesses, one who rode with him to a dinner where they were all night." Blain sipped his coffee. "From the reports, he's very upset and wants to come here, but the locals have suggested he stay away for now. He seems to be unavailable at the moment, however."

"Harry Boston." Rikki's frown said it all. "I'm surprised he hasn't come looking for me. He'd want answers."

"You don't like him?"

"He hangs out with Chad a lot and reports back with whatever he can drag out of Tessa about me. Or he did." She shrugged and played with the zipper on her jacket, a deep sadness moving through her eyes. "He always seemed a tad shady to me. But I couldn't tell Tessa that. She loved him."

"Would he murder for Chad?"

She shook her head. "He wouldn't kill Tessa. He truly loved her. I'm sure he's devastated but since you won't let me talk to him, I have no way of knowing what he's thinking."

"You don't need to call anyone connected to this case. For your own safety."

"Harry didn't approve of Tessa and I being so close."

"But you two were close before he came into the picture, right?"

"Yes, before Chad or Harry either one came into the picture. Why is it that men are so needy? Always wanting us to themselves?"

Blain did a mock frown and glanced behind

him as if she were talking to someone else. "Is that a rhetorical question?"

"Of course it is," she said. "Besides, you don't strike me as the needy type. Dark and brooding and dangerous, yes. But then that sounds so cliché, doesn't it?"

She was making him forget why he came here. "Hey, I'm the one asking the questions, okay?"

"And another typical male tactic. A nonanswer."

"Let's go back to Chad and Harry," he said with a slight grin to hide his discomfort. "Do you think they could be off somewhere together, like on a fishing trip or maybe a business deal?"

"Chad and Harry liked to hang out all the time without us, so yes, that is a possibility. Long weekend or something. Chad might have taken Harry off to help him through this. They hated it when Tessa and I would go shopping or if we planned a girls' weekend."

"A weekend kind of like this weekend?"

"Yes. But Tessa assured me that Harry didn't mind her coming to meet me here. And again, he wouldn't have done this. Not to Tessa."

"Maybe he thought she was you?"

"He'd know Tessa." She shook her head. "I just can't see him doing this. He might not be on my top-ten list but I know he loved her. They were planning to get married next year." She stared at the fireplace. "He might show up here yet."

"What kind of things would the boys say to you about your girls' night and other such stuff?"

"Stay home. Let's go out. Why do you need more shoes?" She shook her head. "None of that matter now, does it?"

"It does if they're the jealous type. Domestic violence isn't pretty."

"It's never gone that far," she said. "Well, Chad's come close, which is why I got away from him."

Blain cataloged that comment for the future. "What does Chad do for a living?"

She frowned and tossed ribbons of hair off her shoulders. "He owns several restaurants in Miami and a couple in Tallahassee."

"So he's successful in his own right?"

"Yes. No, he does not hope to get his hands on any Alvanetti money if that's what you're asking."

Blain let that one slide. "And Harry?"

"Harry works in finance. He likes to take other people's money and make even more for them and himself."

Blain made a note of that. He tried to stay focused but all that hair falling around her shoulders kept distracting him. And that cute lounge outfit only added to that distraction. She was a petite little dynamo who'd withheld information—good intentions but bad judgment.

Shouldn't he hold that against her?

Yes, he reminded himself. "I need a list of any other acquaintances that might have had a grudge against you or Tessa. Anybody you'd had words with, or had a run-in with."

"Okay." She got up and found a pen and paper. "Starting now with you?"

He ignored her little joke. "Yes, and going back as far as you can remember."

"I… I don't think I have any known enemies," she said. "I work hard and I've built up a strong client base around the entire state. I've never had a client turn on me, mainly because I'm willing to redo anything that isn't right or that they don't like."

Blain put down his phone and notebook and decided to try some small talk for a few minutes. "Tell me about your work."

She shrugged. "I decorate houses. I like beach themes with a bit of understated elegance. Not too much of any one thing and not too kitschy."

"Yes, too much of any one thing can be dangerous."

She pushed at her fringe of bangs and gave him a daring stare. "Or boring."

Blain couldn't imagine anything this woman

did as boring. "Could you have seen something or heard something that might put you in danger?"

"I don't think so." She hesitated and then added, "But I do deal in a lot of priceless art and antiques."

"Now we're getting some ideas," he said.

"But murder?" She looked pale and unsettled.

"Yes, murder."

"So now my career is in jeopardy?"

He nodded and refocused. "And you're comfortable financially?"

Her dark eyebrows winged up in two perfect slants. "Isn't that a bit too personal?"

"Yes. But that's the point."

She shot up off the couch. "You aren't making any sense, Detective Kent."

"None of this makes sense," Blain countered. "I have to look at every angle. Did someone have a grudge against either of you? Did someone want to steal from either of you or take you hostage in exchange for millions of dollars in ransom? Did you order a priceless antique or doodad that someone wanted? Is this some kind of vendetta against your family? Or Tessa's? Who would follow you here and kill another woman who looks almost exactly like you? And why?"

"I don't know," she said, tears forming in her

dark eyes. "I've told you over and over that I don't know. I came here to visit my mother and I also planned to use the time to get my head on straight and finally get over Chad. Tessa wanted to visit with me and have some fun. I… I needed my best friend and so she came."

She shrugged, hugged herself as she stood in front of the fire. "That's all I know. I hoped to get some work done for clients who have summer homes in the area too—mainly to give me something to do that would distract me from all my problems."

Blain held firm against her misty gaze and resisted the need to tug her close and comfort her. He didn't do comfort very well. "I'll need a list of those client names."

"My clients aren't killers," she retorted.

"Anyone can become a killer for any kind of reason," Blain replied. "Anyone."

They heard a door open and then a shuffling set of footsteps coming from the hallway from the garage. Blain stood up, prepared for a guard coming to tell him he needed to leave.

But this man was not a guard.

"What's going on here?" Franco Alvanetti stopped just inside the kitchen, his hostile gaze scorching Blain with disdain.

Rikki's gaze locked with Blain's in what might have been a warning and then she turned to face her father. "The detective is following up with some more questions for me, Papa."

"Detective Kent, does my daughter need a good lawyer?" Franco asked, his hands in the pockets of his expensive trousers, his frown etched in fatigue and overindulgence.

Blain gave Rikki a questioning stare and then met her father's disapproving frown. "Not yet, sir."

Rikki wanted to drop off the face of the earth. Her father and the law—not good in one room together. And especially not good with this one. Blain had that I-won't-back-down attitude perfected. The clinched fists, the daring solid wall of an expression and the buff body braced for action.

Lots of action.

She shouldn't be attracted to a man who hated her family and had her on a suspect list. But there it was, plain and simple. Instead of wanting him to leave, Rikki just wanted to protect him from her father's wrath.

As if Blain Kent needed protecting.

"It's okay, Papa," she said to prove that point. "I can handle this."

"Can you, really?" her father asked. "You've brought danger to your sick mother's door. After refusing to associate with this family for years, you decide to come home and bring murder with you. I'll never understand you, Regina."

"That's enough," Blain said.

Rikki blinked away the raw pain that made her eyes swell with moisture and turned to find Blain standing by her side. "Your daughter is co-operating with us in every aspect of this investigation. Whoever did this also came after her last night. And regardless of how I feel, that's why she's staying here." He glanced around and pointed a finger at Franco. "You have a fortress here so even I agree this is the best place for her right now. Unless you want something terrible to happen to her, too."

Rikki expected her father to tell Blain to get out of his house. Instead, he took a deep breath and stared over at Blain with puffy eyes and a deep, puckered brow. "Do you think the killer mistook Tessa to be my daughter?"

"I do, sir," Blain said, his arm brushing against Rikki's like a warning caress. "But I can't give you a conclusive comment on that yet. Rikki is going to put together a list of everyone she's talked to or worked with over the last few weeks. And in the meantime, I'll keep in touch with the Miami and Tallahassee authorities and see what we can come up with."

Franco moved into the big den, his power

practically radiating off his body. "You will keep me informed."

Blain's expression looked like jagged ice. "I don't usually keep anyone outside the department informed on an active case, sir."

"But you'll make an exception."

Blain's body went rigid again. He braced his legs apart and crossed his arms over his chest, the rustle of his leather jacket sending out "keep off" vibes. "I don't make exceptions, Mr. Alvanetti."

Her father actually looked nonplussed and confused. Rikki seriously wanted to kiss Blain Kent. Nobody ever talked back to her father.

Then she realized she wouldn't mind kissing Blain Kent, regardless of her father. Which would only make things worse for both of them.

Franco sank down in his favorite leather chair and uttered a tired sigh. "So we have a dead woman who was found at my daughter's home. Her best friend, Tessa Jones, who just happens to resemble her. Interesting, isn't it?"

Did he even care? Rikki wondered.

"Very interesting," Blain said. "The whole town is buzzing with scenarios. Which is why I don't want to release the details. Brings out a lot of wackos and wannabe-snitches."

Franco patted the cushy arms of the chair with his meaty hands. "I see." He coughed and cleared his throat. "I will make sure my daughter is safe while you do your job."

Her father nodded. A dismissal.

Rikki breathed a sigh of her own and motioned to Blain. "I'll show you out, Detective Kent."

Blain gave her a surprised glance but followed her. He stopped near her father's chair. "I want to find the person who did this so I hope you understand. And I hope you'll trust me."

"I do not trust easily," Franco replied, his gaze on the roaring fire.

Blain didn't move. "Neither do I."

"Let's go," Rikki said, almost a plea.

Blain put his hands in the pockets of his jacket and followed her toward the side door to the garage.

When they were outside, he turned to her. "I know a threat when I hear one but I'm okay with that. But you need to understand something, Rikki."

She shivered in the wind. "And what's that?"

"I'm trying to protect you, so don't do anything stupid, okay?"

"I'll try not to," Rikki retorted, anger warming her now. "I plan to stay right here and visit my mother while I try to get some work done."

"Good plan." He looked sheepish. Swiping

at his hair, he glanced over at her. "At least you have a nice place to stay hidden."

"Yes, a virtual paradise," she quipped. "A comfortable prison."

"Is that what it feels like?" he asked, his gaze tearing at her with his unspoken questions.

"It's always felt that way but I try not to complain. I have everything here I could ever possibly need, except freedom."

He drew closer and touched at her hair. "Hey, I know this has been tough and I'm sorry I've had to drill you. But I have a job to do."

Before she could pull away or respond, he leaned closer, his eyes as dark as driftwood at midnight. "But you call me anytime, you hear? Anytime."

Then he dropped his hand and walked to his car.

And left her there shivering in the wind again.

SEVEN

Blain went back over the list Rikki had emailed him late yesterday. She had several high-profile clients in the area, including one of Blain's best friends, Alec Caldwell.

Deciding to be completely transparent with Alec, Blain dialed Alec's number and waited. When Alec came on the line, Blain went right into action. "Hey, man. Listen, I'm going over a client list for Regina Alvanetti and I noticed you're on it."

Alec chuckled. "And how are you today, Detective Kent?"

"Sorry," Blain said, rubbing the throbbing nerve in his forehead. "I can't talk much about it but I guess you're familiar with this case I'm working on, right?"

"Oh, yes. Aunt Hattie and her friends are all concerned they'll be next. They read the papers and listen to the news on a constant basis. Should I be worried?"

"I don't think so. This appears to be more of a calculated hit than a random robbery. But that is not for public knowledge, especially not for Aunt-Hattie-type public knowledge. But please reassure your aunt that she and her friends certainly need to be alert and cautious but to go about their regular activities."

"Got it," Alec replied. "I'm sorry about the woman who was murdered. And to answer your question, yes, Aunt Hattie and I consulted with Rikki when we were redoing some of the rooms at Caldwell House and Marla and I asked her to help with some sketches for our wedding décor. She sent her ideas free of charge and let our wedding planner take over from there since she wasn't sure she could make it back for the wedding. She's good at her job."

"This isn't about her job but more about anyone she's worked with," Blain said. "I'm going down a list of her clients, calling people to see if anyone might be upset with her."

"I can't answer to that but I can vouch for Rikki," Alec said. "She's a good person, Blain. She tries to keep her nose clean and she only comes back here to see her mother every so often. You probably know this already but Sonia has been ill for months now." He paused and then added, "By the way, maybe Rikki will be at the wedding. If she's up to it after what she's been through."

Blain glanced at the calendar. "You're getting married in two weeks. Wow, that's soon."

Alec went silent and then asked, "Uh…you will be there, right?"

Blain had to smile at Alec being a nervous groom. "I'm your best man, so yes, I'm planning on being there."

Although if Rikki Alvanetti came to the wedding, he'd be nervous, too. For all of them.

"Just checking," Alec replied. "I know how it works with you detective types."

"I'll be there," Blain said again, making a big red reminder on his calendar. "Got measured for my fancy suit and everything. Might even get my hair trimmed. And we have your bachelor party out at the camp next week. I'll surely be there."

"Nothing fancy," Alec replied. "And no tricks."

"Don't worry. Preacher will keep us on the straight and narrow."

"Always."

Blain went over his notes. "So can you think of anyone who'd want to hurt Rikki? Did you know her friend Tessa?"

"I didn't know Tessa," Alec said. "But I do know that Rikki's family has made some enemies over the years. But most of those people tend to undercut business deals or take away clients. I can't imagine any of them killing an innocent young woman."

"But if the hit man thought that woman was Regina Alvanetti?"

That's a whole 'nother matter," Alec said. "And a hard case to crack."

"Tell me about it," Blain retorted. "Thanks, Alec. I'll talk to you soon. Tell Marla I said hello."

He hung up and called a few more of the names on the list. Most of the clients only had good things to say about her so no one stood out.

But any one of these people could put on a good act for a stranger asking questions. She'd said she had a few appointments while she was here. He'd need to go over that schedule, too. She might need to cancel those meetings. Or he could go with her to all of them and observe. And protect her while he was at it.

He'd also do background checks on as many clients as he could. Even wealthy people could turn out to be criminals. Happened all the time.

He probably needed to talk to her neighbors again. People around that complex had to have heard something or seen something. He'd send one of the uniformed officers out again since Blain liked to keep a low profile.

But this was Millbrook, after all. Everyone knew everyone else. And that could hinder this case.

Deciding to call and check on Rikki, Blain walked outside to get some fresh air. He'd had the slashed tire replaced and he'd asked a couple of the patrolmen to watch the parking lot. Could be a random thing—kids out for a dare or maybe someone else who had a beef with him.

But Blain's gut told him that tire had been slashed deliberately. Was the killer still hanging around?

He gazed around the parking lot while he waited for Rikki to pick up.

"Hello."

Her low, husky voice took away some of the December chill. "Hi. It's Blain Kent. Just checking in. How are things going today?"

"My mother is awake," she said. "A good sign but she's still disoriented. Everything else is okay."

She didn't sound okay. "Are you sure?"

When she didn't speak, he let out a breath. "Rikki, I need you to be honest with me. I can't protect you if you keep hiding things from me."

"I'm not hiding anything," she said. "Tessa's boyfriend, Harry, called me this morning. I planned on telling you but I've been fielding client calls all morning, too."

"And you took the call from Harry?"

"Yes. I thought it was one of my client's numbers. He just needed to talk." She went silent and then said, "He sounded sincerely upset but he told me he was out with clients the night she died. I believe him. He wants to bring her body back to Tallahassee for burial."

"We can work that out later," Blain said. "Did he happen to mention dear ol' Chad?"

"No. And neither did I."

"I'm coming out there," Blain said, deciding he might need to set up a monitor on her phone calls. Someone could have a GPS tracker on her phone. "I'm at the station but I'll be there in a few minutes."

"You don't need to do that," she said. "I'm okay, really. I didn't talk to him for long."

"I'm still coming out there." He hung up and got in his car. He didn't really need to see her face-to-face but he wanted to see her. Face-to-face.

Wishing he had more willpower, Blain wondered why this particular woman had to be the one who'd finally gotten to him. He'd rather deal with a deranged junkie than an Alvanetti, but this particular Alvanetti wasn't so horrible to be around.

Who was he to question? Preacher always said things happened in God's own time. Blain hit the gas pedal once he was outside the city limits and wondered why God had chosen to test him by forcing him to protect an Alvanetti from a killer.

A lot of irony in that.

Preacher also said God had a good sense of humor at times.

He found her in the stables.

"What are you doing?"

Rikki turned from saddling a gleaming black horse that had to be worth more than he'd made in five years. She wore tall brown leather boots and riding pants with a silvery-colored down vest over a black turtleneck.

"I needed to get some air," she said. "I have two guards with me." She motioned to the shadows where two hulking figures stood.

Blain studied the two suits. "And they'll follow you on foot? Or do they have tricycles?"

She shook her head and smiled. "They have a golf cart."

And big guns.

He stared down the stalls. "Do you have an extra horse around here?"

She glanced over at him. "Why?"

"I'm riding with you."

"I don't think—"

"I said I'm riding with you and we're staying near the corral."

She motioned again and a groom materialized from yet another shadowy corner. After asking the young man to saddle Rambo, she turned back to Blain. "I hope you know *how* to ride, Detective."

"I do."

It had been a while but it had to be like riding a bike. Only a horse named Rambo couldn't be docile.

Blain pushed away his trepidations and studied the stables. "It's too dark in here. Don't come out here at night even with your two buddies."

"I won't."

She checked her horse, cooing. "Daisy, this is Detective Blain Kent. He can be intimidating and grumpy but don't let that fool you. He's actually a nice person."

The black mare shook her mane and eyed Blain with a feminine regard.

He was getting more and more nervous by the minute. And he didn't do nervous. But she was deliberately putting herself in danger by going out into the open. Even iron gates and strong fences couldn't stop a bullet. Which is why he'd have to be on alert while she took some air.

When the young groom came around the corner with a giant red roan stallion, Blain stood back to stare. "Really?"

"Really," she said with a grin. "He's as tame as a kitten."

"Right." He wagged a finger at her. "If I get thrown—"

"We'll load you onto the golf cart."

Blain wouldn't cower. She'd like that. If getting on this giant beast meant he could watch out for her then he'd do it.

He just hoped they'd be safe. If anything happened to her on his watch, her father would have Blain shot on the spot.

Rikki glanced back at the man riding Rambo. Maybe she shouldn't have saddled Blain on her brother's favorite stallion but she figured the detective needed a horse to match his own dominating personality. And he did look good sitting there with a certain ease that probably belied his initial concerns.

"How you doing?" she called, aware of the golf cart keeping a discreet distance behind them. Although they were circling the enclosed pasture near the stables, at least she was out getting some fresh air.

Blain nudged Rambo along beside her. "I'm fine. Never better. That wind off the water is cold and I'm sure I'll be so sore tomorrow I won't be able to walk. Plus, I'm trying to see through the trees past that elaborate fence, just in case someone might be out there waiting to shoot at you."

Rikki's heart did that little lurch. The pang of horror and fear that hit her each time she thought about Tessa settled over her like a fog. "I thought getting out of the house might help but…it's always there. The image of my friend laying there, the blood, the vacant stare in her eyes." She pulled Daisy up underneath a towering live oak and dismounted. "You sure are a buzzkill, Detective."

He followed her and tied the horses on a low hanging branch of the big tree. "I'm sorry but I have to keep reminding you that this isn't over."

Rikki turned away from him. Out here away from the shoreline, the wind whipped against the trees in a mournful wail that only reminded her of how close to that edge of hysteria she'd been over the last few days. She should have stayed inside with her mother but Franco was home and roaming around like a lost puppy. She didn't know what to say to her father.

"I understand but I'm not comfortable in this house."

"Hey." Blain turned her around, his eyes like a dark ocean. "I don't want the same thing to happen to you. I believe you don't know who killed Tessa but we don't know why someone came after you that same night. So, yes…you're still in danger."

Rikki glanced back to where the golf cart had stopped by a patch of scrub oaks near the back of the big barn. "I know and I feel guilty, trying to do normal things. I think I'm still in shock." She glanced up at Blain. He stood a foot or so away but his expression seemed so intimate and close. Too intimate. Too close.

Rikki wanted to run into his arms and let his warmth surround her. Instead, she stared out over the pasture. "I love riding. I was pretty good in the junior rodeo competition when I was younger."

Blain's dark expression softened. "You…a rodeo star?"

"Me," she said, those good memories clouding out the sad ones. "I won the barrel-racing competition three years in a row and I finaled in calf and goat roping."

"Goat roping?" His smile warmed her to her toes. "Wow, you're just full of surprises."

Rikki wondered if that had been meant as a compliment or a condemnation. "But you don't like surprises, right?"

He gave her a steady blue-eyed stare. "I like good surprises. What I don't like is duplicity and…insincerity."

"Wow, you're just full of gloom."

"I am," he said. "You know, I'm marine all the way. I was an MP toward the end of my last deployment. So call me a skeptic but I've seen the worst of people."

She should have known he was a warrior. He carried himself in that way, all gung ho and tough, never willing to back down. "Do you ever look for the best first?"

"No," he said. "Or at least, I never did before."

Rikki watched him. He didn't keep his gaze fixed on any one thing. He was always checking, always scanning the horizon as if he were still in warrior mode. But the way he'd said that gave her hope that he might be slowly coming around on things. That he might be able to look past her name and see her heart.

"So you're a hero," she said, thinking the layers beneath that dark gaze were deep. She'd love to explore those layers, maybe peel back a few barriers.

"Some might say that." He turned and glanced back at the two guards. "But not every soldier is a hero."

Rikki moved to block him and force him to look at her. "And not every Alvanetti is a criminal."

"Duly noted," he said. Then he leaned close. "You certainly don't look like a criminal to me."

Rikki could feel the heat from his body. If

she moved a few inches closer, she could reach out and kiss Blain. He must have felt the same way. She saw a flare of awareness in his eyes and then—

And then the echo of a gun blast shattered the countryside and scared the horses into a frenzied dance. Blain did pull her close. He grabbed her and whirled her around behind the trunk of the big tree and held her there, his weapon trained on the woods.

EIGHT

Blain heard another shot and watched as one of the guards hit the ground. The other one managed to get behind the golf cart.

"I knew this was a bad idea," he said, his hand holding Rikki's head. "You're too exposed out here."

"The horses." She tried to turn but Blain held her tight.

"They'll be okay. You need to stay down."

Daisy decided she didn't like the situation. She broke loose and took off toward the stables.

Rambo whinnied and snorted, his hoofs kicking dirt as if ready for battle.

"They've hit one of your men," Blain said. He watched the woods past the fence line. Someone had to be up in a tree with a high-powered rifle.

Rikki gulped a breath, her gaze on the golf cart. "You're right. Bad idea. I thought I'd be safe here."

"You'd think but someone is determined."

He leaned around the tree. His Glock wouldn't do much except hold them off until he could come up with a plan.

The other guard motioned to him and pointed toward a stand of tall pines just past the fence line. Blain studied the woods and saw a glint, just a quick blink but enough that Blain got a bead on the shooter. Not enough to move in, but at least a location.

Had someone been waiting for such an opportunity?

He held Rikki and nodded. "Okay, I think I know where they're coming from but I need you to stay behind this tree for a minute."

"And what are you going to do?"

"I'm going to cover your man who has a military-grade machine gun. And I'm hoping he'll cover us until I can get you back to the stables."

She nodded, her eyes wide. "Okay."

Blain nodded to the guard and managed to sign what he needed. "Call for reinforcements," he mouthed.

The guard pulled out a walkie-talkie and spoke into it.

Blain waited until the call had gone out then pushed Rikki behind him. "If that doesn't work or no one comes soon, I'm gonna put you on Rambo and send you home."

"Not without you," she said.

"We'll argue about that later," he replied.

Then he leaned out from behind the tree and was rewarded with a sharp ping that hit the trunk and scattered bark six inches from his head. Blain returned fire and so did the guard.

The woods went silent after that.

"He's not going to give up," Blain said. "If we do get reinforcements, they could get shot, too." He pulled out his phone. "I'll have to call in the sheriff's department and give them a location of the shooter or we could be pinned down all day."

Blain had to make the call since they were outside the city limits, but his dad would hear that call on the scanner he still kept active by his recliner. Sam Kent might be retired but once a sheriff, always a sheriff.

"I'm sorry, Blain," she said, her voice low.

"For what?"

"For not listening to you. For insisting on leaving the house."

He gave her a forgiving glance. "And I'm sorry for not making you stay inside. So there, we're even."

He tried to move again and almost got hit.

"Okay, he's settling in." Blain pulled Rikki down beside him behind the three-foot tree trunk. "Which means we will, too."

She shivered. "Maybe we should send Rambo back. It's not that far. He knows the way and besides, you kept me so close to the stables, I could make a run for it, too."

"Daisy has sent out one alert, arriving without a rider," he said. "Rambo seems okay. And you are not going anywhere, understand?"

"My brother won't like that I took out his horse."

"Your brother? This horse belongs to your brother?"

"Yes."

"Great."

She shivered again and Blain tugged her into his arms to warm her. "You're determined to drive me nuts, aren't you?"

She looked down at her boots. "If you get me back home, I'll be a model citizen from here on out."

"Right." He nuzzled her hair and inhaled the spicy scent that always seemed to surround her. "We'll get you out of this, one way or another, Rikki."

An hour later, the whole thing was over.

Rikki stood near the stables and held back yet more tears. One of her father's most trusted guards was dead. The other one was shaken but he'd managed to hold off the shooter until several other bodyguards found them and got

Rikki and that guard into an SUV with bullet-proof windows.

While she'd watched Blain out the window trying to cover them.

"We can't leave him," she told the driver. She could hear gunshots echoing over the woods.

"I got my orders from your father," the man shouted.

"Then stop and let me out," she screamed, her hand on the door.

The men looked at each other and then back to Rikki. "We have our orders."

"I will not go unless you help Detective Kent, too," she said. "And if I get out and get shot, you'll have to explain that."

They circled back for Blain. He managed to send Rambo home and then he hopped in beside her without a word. So much for going for a peaceful horseback ride.

By the time they arrived back at the house, her brother Santo was waiting, raging at anyone who'd listen.

"You are something, you know that?" he shouted to Rikki before she could approach Blain. "I get a call that it was like a war zone out here. What's the deal with you, Rikki?"

Blain managed to materialize beside her. "The deal is that your sister is being stalked by a killer," he said, pulling Rikki behind him. "Why won't anyone around here take that seriously?"

"Then why did she leave the house?" Santo asked, his dark eyes flashing fire. He was a younger version of their father but he had not married a woman like her mother. His own wife hated him. So he was always growling and raging at someone.

Before Rikki could speak, Blain put out his hand. "It's my fault. I... I told her I'd go with her and keep her safe."

"Well, you didn't do a very good job," Santo said, pointing a finger at Blain. "Typical of the Millbrook Police Department." He nodded toward the hired help. "This is why we have to pay people to protect us."

Rikki came around Blain. She wanted to tell her brother they had to hire guards because they might be involved in criminal activities. But she didn't say that since she didn't have any proof.

"He's doing everything in his power," she told Santo. "I wanted to go for a ride and he felt obligated to go with me."

Santo's scowl grew. "Aren't you two just all cozy?"

"Enough."

They all turned to find her father standing there with a man Rikki recognized as the former sheriff. She couldn't remember his name since she'd avoided any friend of her father's whenever she was in this house. But he looked familiar.

Blain and Santo both glanced toward her father.

"Let them alone," Franco said. "Rikki, go inside and calm down."

Santo shut up but he stood with his hands on his hips.

Blain stared at the sheriff. "Sir."

The older man looked as angry as her father and brother. "We caught the shooter. He's being held in the county jail if you want a go at him."

"I do want a go at him," Blain said, his expression grim.

Her father stepped forward. "Rikki, do you remember Sheriff Kent?"

"I believe so." Rikki looked at the sheriff and then she looked at Blain. "Kent?"

"He's my father," Blain said, his tone level and full of resentment.

"Your father." She couldn't believe this but it made sense now. "I see I'm not the only one who's been keeping secrets." Giving Blain one last glance, she turned toward the house.

She should have known she didn't need to trust a determined detective.

An hour later, Blain found Rikki in the kitchen staring at the microwave. When she heard him come in, she glanced up at him and then opened the microwave to pull out a bowl of soup.

"Rikki—"

"I have to take this to my mother," she said. "Daphne had to run some errands."

He braced his hands against the granite counter. "I'll wait for you, then."

"You don't need to do that."

"I'll be here, waiting," he said.

She ignored him and carried a tray down the long hallway toward the back of the house.

Blain stood in front of the fireplace. The afternoon had turned chilly and windy and all he wanted was a hot shower and his own bowl of soup before he went to sleep on his couch. But it would be hours before he could get any sleep.

When he heard a door slamming, Blain turned to find his father with Franco and Santo Alvanetti. The three men each gave him a pointed stare.

"I'm going to check on Mama," Santo said, his black-eyed frown clearly blaming Blain for this latest turn of events.

"Would you and your son like something to drink, maybe some coffee?" Franco asked Sam after Santo stalked away.

"I'm fine," Blain said, eyeing the hallway to the other wing of the house. He hoped Santo didn't start in on Rikki.

"And I have to go," Sam said. "I'm sure my son will want to get to the sheriff substation to question our shooter. Sorry about your man, Franco."

Franco nodded. "Comes with the territory."

Blain wanted to punch the wall. The territory? A way of life that involved illegal activities and possible killings—and blaming his only daughter for being in the wrong place at the wrong time?

Any reservations he'd had about helping Rikki dissolved right along with the ash floating up from the fire. No wonder the woman had gotten away and no wonder she couldn't trust anyone.

Especially anyone like him.

He glanced toward the hallway again then looked at his father. Sam stared at him with that smug, condescending expression he remembered so well, growing up.

"I'm going," Blain announced to the room. He'd talk to Rikki later. "Sorry about what happened, Mr. Alvanetti. But maybe we can get the shooter to talk."

Franco's frown deepened into a craggy rock face. "If you don't make him talk, I will."

Blain shook his head and pinched his nose with two fingers. "Getting a suspect to talk is my job, Mr. Alvanetti. Not yours."

"I'll sit in, if my son will allow me," Sam said.

Blain started for the door. "Your jurisdiction, your call."

Franco chuckled at that. "I knew who you were the day you showed up here," he said to Blain. "But you're different from Sam here."

Blain looked from Franco to his father. "Yeah, I am."

Then he turned and left the room.

"Mama, you need to eat some soup," Rikki said, her mind in turmoil. She wanted to get away from here, to leave and never come back but Sonia needed her. And today of all days, her mother was lucid and willing to sit up.

"I'm not that hungry," Sonia said, a skinny hand patting her bun.

"But you're sitting up today," Rikki replied, holding the tray so her mother wouldn't tip the hot soup over on herself. "That's a good sign."

Pebble ambled into the bedroom and jumped on her mother's bed. Sonia giggled and reached out a hand to pet the cat.

Santo stomped into the room. "Hey, Mama. I see you're wearing your pretty bed jacket."

Sonia's smile widened. "Santo, what are you doing here? Shouldn't you be at work?"

Santo glared at Rikki and then gave Sonia a kiss on the cheek. Pebble protested and hissed then leaped off the bed. "I'm just checking up on y'all. I worry."

Rikki heard the condemnation in that statement. She would never understand why her best friend being killed had somehow brought more shame on this family than any of her brothers' or even her father's shenanigans. Did they all know something she wasn't aware of?

"Everyone here is fine," Sonia said. She obediently took a spoonful of soup. "Rikki is home for Christmas, you know. I'm gonna get out of this bed and we'll bake and decorate and listen to Christmas music, won't we Rikki-pie?"

Rikki swallowed the lump in her throat and nodded. "We sure will, Mama. But right now, you need to take your medicine and rest. You did pretty good on the soup."

"I am a bit tired," Sonia replied. She winked at her son. "Y'all are so darlin', always fussing over me and checking on me. I'll be better tomorrow."

"Yes, you will," Rikki said, praying for that to be so.

Her sweet mother said this almost every day or at least on her good days. Today was a good day for Sonia even while it had turned out to be a bad day for everyone else.

Rikki cleaned up her mother and after moving the tray she gave Sonia a kiss. "I'm going to the kitchen. Santo is still here."

Her brother gave her another look of dismissal. "And I'll always be right here."

And another biting comment that hit Rikki right through the heart. She hoped Blain had left by now. She wasn't ready to deal with him again today.

His father was a retired sheriff. The man who used to hang around her father like a puppy, always smiling and waiting for handouts. How could she have forgotten so soon?

But she reminded herself that she'd tried to avoid her father's cronies and she'd only seen the imposing sheriff from a distance most days.

But she knew he must have taken kickbacks and bribes from her father since he hadn't made any arrests when she was growing up. It had been obvious today that Sam Kent and his son didn't see eye to eye.

Blain was so different from most of the men she knew. He was good. She could see that. So why did it hurt so much to know he hadn't told her who his father was? Especially when he'd criticized her for withholding her real identity from him?

No wonder he hated her family. His father and her father, together, doing who knew what. She and Blain had grown up in much the same way, but on different sides of the fence. It was enough to make her sick to her stomach.

But when she thought about how he'd held her there by the old oak, she had to close her eyes and take a breath. He'd told her he'd get her out of this, one way or another. Rikki didn't want Blain to get killed trying to save her.

When she got to the kitchen, that room and the big adjoining den were both empty. Blain and his father must have left. Where was Daphne? That nurse didn't do nearly the job that Peggy did.

And where was her father?

The intercom buzzed while she was giving Pebble a treat. Thinking it might be Santo or her mother, Rikki answered. "Yes?"

"Come into my office," Franco said. "We need to talk."

Rikki took a calming breath. "I'll be right there, Papa."

She figured she was about to get a lecture.

Well, she could handle it for her mother's sake.

She would have to handle all of this and survive so she could leave again, one way or another. After all, she'd been doing that for years now.

Running away.

Always running away.

NINE

Rikki knocked on the double doors to her father's study and steeled herself against his wrath. She'd get through this and then she'd go and sit with her mother since Santo had finally left.

"Come in."

She opened the doors and saw her father standing by the mantel staring into the fireplace. This place had several fireplaces and usually they were all decorated for the holidays. But without her mother's organized supervision, no one had bothered bringing out the rest of the decorations. Maybe she could do that, to keep herself busy.

After she shut the door, Franco turned around and motioned to the sitting area by the fire. "I have coffee and hot tea if you'd like any." He pointed to the coffee table. "And some sandwiches. You need to eat."

Wondering why her father was being so

solicitous, Rikki shook her head. "I'm not hungry but thank you."

Franco finally sat down and took up his cup of coffee. "I'm sorry for the things your brother said to you earlier."

"Really?" Shocked, Rikki decided maybe she did need some hot tea, after all. "I've had the feeling since I've been home that nothing I've done has pleased any of you."

"You're wrong on that," Franco said, lowering his head. "Listen, I've been angry at you for a long time. First, you marry that boy—"

"I loved him."

"You used him to get away from me."

Rikki's heart cracked at that comment. "No, I loved Drake. We wanted to have a life together but...you had him killed."

Her father lifted his head, his eyes red-rimmed and fatigued. "What are you talking about?"

"You can tell me the truth," she said. "I know you had him killed but everyone thinks it was an accident. I had to leave after that, Papa. I... I couldn't stay here. And I'll leave again as soon as this is over."

Franco sat his coffee cup down so hard the rich liquid slapped over the sides. "I did not have Drake Allen killed." He pushed a hand down his face. "The boy was drunk that night, Regina. He liked to party when you thought he was working.

He ran off the road and died in a car crash. That is the truth."

She'd heard that same story over and over. But she'd never believe it. "Why did you ask me to come in here?"

Her father stared at her, his eyes still misty. "You are so like your mother. She wanted us to make peace, you and me. I want that but I get so angry and I lash out and I hurt people."

"Atonement, Papa? Is that what this is about? You want me to forgive you in case Mama dies?"

"She will not die," Franco said. "She can't die."

And then Rikki saw it there in her father's old eyes.

Fear.

Franco Alvanetti was afraid of the one thing he couldn't control. Losing his wife.

Rikki got up, her own eyes burning. "She's getting better and I'll stay to make sure she does."

Then she turned and left the room, her heart splitting as she waged anger and bitterness against acceptance and forgiveness.

Blain came out of the interrogation room located in the back of the district substation not far from the Alvanetti estate. The SWAT and K-9 teams had cornered the shooter in the woods near the state park that ran along the bay.

That meant television cameras and reporters pushing microphones in his face. People wanted answers and Blain had none to give. Yet.

Blain had gone in with a deputy to question John Darty. Fun name for a fun criminal.

"You're a piece of work, Darty," Blain said by way of a greeting. "Drug charges, stolen property, petty crimes. Seems you just got out and now you'll be going right back in."

"I want a lawyer."

The man was trained in weaponry, courtesy of the United States Army. As Blain had told Rikki, not every soldier was a hero. This soldier had gone quiet and now refused to speak. Not surprising. Whoever had sent him would probably try to kill him if he talked, in or out of a jailhouse.

"Think long and hard about telling us who hired you," he told the fidgety man. "We can help you now but once you go back inside, it might be too late."

Sam Kent was waiting for Blain in the conference room.

"Things sure have changed since my day," his father said, glancing around. "Districts, SWAT teams, even a Major Crimes Unit. Used to be just a sheriff and several deputies."

"This county has become more populated over the last decade, Dad. Not to mention having advanced technology."

"Job never gets any easier," Sam said on a grunt. "What did our guest reveal?"

"Not much," Blain said. "Didn't you listen in?"

"Nope." Sam threw his disposable cup in the trash. "I thought I'd let you do your thing."

"My thing didn't work." Surprised at how docile his usually ornery father seemed, Blain gave Sam the once-over. "Hey, you feeling okay?"

Sam's eyebrows winged up like an eagle in flight. "Fine as a fiddle, thank you."

Blain took a good look at his dad. Sam looked tired. He'd lost weight. Not daring to ask any more questions, Blain decided his cagey father could be as tight-lipped as a career criminal at times.

So he tried another method. "What do you think?"

"About what?" Sam asked.

"This case." Blain ran a hand over his hair. "I think Regina Alvanetti is being targeted for a reason and I've got a feeling someone is after her because they think she knows something or she saw something."

"I agree," Sam said, lowering his voice.

"You might consider her family. Lots of hidden agendas going on."

Surprised yet again, Blain gave his father a thoughtful stare. "Do you know something I need to know?"

Sam grinned. "I know a lot of things I've never talked about but I always knew that one day some of those things would float to the surface."

Aggravation slapped at Blain, making him snap. "I'm not sure what you're trying to say."

"Sonia," his father whispered. "Sonia knows more secrets than anyone else."

"But she's ill," Blain replied. "No way I can get to her. She's barely able to get out of bed."

"But you can get to the daughter," Sam said. "That woman trusts you and trust from an Alvanetti is a rare thing."

"She might not trust me now," Blain admitted. "I didn't tell her that I'm your son."

"I kind of gathered that," Sam said. "She'll get past that because she knows you're on her side."

Blain understood but he didn't think Rikki would appreciate him trying to get past her to her mother. "So I get to Sonia through Rikki?"

"Yep." His dad gave him a crystal-eyed stare. "You'll figure it out."

A dozen mixed emotions whirled through

Blain's system. "Why are you changing your tune?"

Sam shot him a long stare and then waved his hand in the air. "Like you said, this whole county has changed over the last few years. You need to understand, the Alvanetti family has changed, too. A new guard has taken over and I've got a feeling what I saw in my day is tame compared to what could be going on now."

Blain wanted to ask his father what exactly he was trying to say but decided he'd had enough shocks for one day. This conversation was the first decent one he'd had with his father in a long time. And yet, he didn't have a clue what was being said.

"Hey, Dad," he called after his father. "What made *you* change?"

Sam stopped, one hand on the glass doors to the parking lot. "Watching you today."

Then he turned and stomped out the door.

"I've got to start back over from square one."

Blain sat back in his chair and stared out at the water. It was raining and cold but he sat with Alec and Preacher out on the screened porch of the camp house they all owned together. An electric heater buzzed nearby and the pizza boxes were now almost empty.

Alec Caldwell gave Blain a blank stare.

"Sounds as if you got more information from your old man than you did from this suspect."

"Yep." Without giving away any details, Blain had told his friends what was common knowledge since it had been blasted all over the airwaves. He'd also told them about the sudden change in his father. "I can't decide where my dad fits in."

Rory Sanderson stood up, his hands in the deep pockets of his fleece jacket. "Your dad's getting on in years, Blain. Maybe he's trying to make amends before it's too late."

"I wish he'd just level with me," Blain said. "I don't need amends right now. I need cold, hard facts."

Rory shot Alec a glance. "He's a lawman like you. Maybe he can't divulge everything he's seen or heard."

"He could be trying to warn you and protect you," Alec offered. "Sure he's stubborn and hard-edged but he loves you. I'd think there was a lot he shielded you and your mother from when he was in charge."

Alec had never known his own dad and because his mother, Vivian, had mourned her military husband's death, she'd been emotionally distant toward Alec. Blain needed to take that into consideration.

"I guess so. I mean, in spite of our differences

he's never once condemned me for anything I've done. Criticized my methods but he never told me I shouldn't do something. He didn't try to talk me out of joining the marines and he didn't even blink when I came home and joined the police force."

"And so he's not saying anything to condemn you now, either," Rory added. He sat back down. "I'll be praying for both of your tonight, that's for sure."

Blain lifted his soft drink in a salute. "Without ceasing."

"And what about Rikki?" Alec asked.

Blain wasn't sure how to respond. She was not taking his calls. "I don't know. I have to find out who's behind this before she gets killed. That's my job."

"We don't want her to get killed," Alec said. "I was asking more along the lines of what about how you *feel* about Rikki?"

Blain lowered his gaze and studied the plastic cup in his hand. "I don't know about that, either. She's a complicated subject."

Rory grinned. "A dangerous subject. You might need to walk away once you're done with this case."

"Worried about me, Preacher?"

"Nope." Rory found a piece of cold pizza.

"Just…bemused. I haven't seen you so besotted before."

"Who says I'm besotted?"

Alec laughed. "Rikki is a beautiful woman. Mysterious and under pressure right now. You're one of the good guys."

"Your point?"

"It all adds up to trouble," Alec finished. "She'll turn to you and you'll do the right thing. Just be careful."

"I thought you had already vouched for her," Blain said.

"I did on a professional basis. And I like Rikki. But you've always avoided getting tangled in a relationship so it's different seeing you so tangled up in this one."

Blain got up and tossed his cup in the trash. "I kind of miss Hunter. The Okie doesn't badger me the way you two do." He shrugged. "He must be deep undercover. He's not returning my calls."

"Hunter *is* on assignment," Rory replied. "I guess I'd better throw in a prayer for him, too. Being a private eye is a whole new set of concerns." He chuckled. "Especially when Hunter's idea of finding answers is to inflict physical pain."

"Several concerns," Alec retorted. "But he was special ops. He does that thing—"

"Slips around without a sound?" Rory asked, grinning.

Alec glanced back over his shoulder. "Yeah, that thing."

"He'll show up, hopefully for your wedding," Rory said, glancing at Alec.

"I hope my best man shows up, too," Alec quipped, grinning at Blain.

"I'll be there, okay." Blain decided he'd had enough. "I'm beat. Think I'll head home."

Rory lifted his hand. "Hey, we didn't mean to get too personal."

Alec chimed in. "It's your business, buddy. I should know to trust you since you're good at your job."

Blain nodded. "I know you mean well. But you both need to remember something about me. I may be a bit besotted, but I'm not stupid."

Rory bobbed his head. "And stay not stupid, okay?"

"Always."

He waved to them and headed down to the open garage underneath the house on stilts. He wasn't stupid but he had to make sure Rikki was all right. Did that make him crazy?

Probably.

He got his phone out and hit her number. He didn't like the way they'd left things. They'd been through a lot together since the night he'd seen her on the boardwalk.

And she had to still be reeling from what had happened this morning. He told himself checking on her was the right thing to do.

Just in case she needed someone to talk to tonight.

Rikki wished she had someone to talk to. She'd been so tired by the day's events she'd come to her room right after dinner, taken a hot shower and was now trying to read. Pebble lay spread out in a long cat stretch by her feet. Rikki had tried telling her tale to the cat, but Pebble had become so bored he'd taken to licking his paws and grooming himself.

A sure sign of total disregard.

Her mother, always her first source and the best confidante a girl could have, was sleeping. And even if she were awake, Rikki couldn't bother her mother when she was so sick. If Sonia knew what was going on, she's worry even more.

But then, Sonia Alvanetti never seemed to worry about anything. Her faith held tight against so many things.

Rikki thought of Tessa. Her best friend. Gone. They'd never get to stay up late again, eating chocolate and watching romantic comedies. No more going shopping at cluttered boutiques and having cheesecake for dessert. No more trips to places all over the south and sometimes out of the country. No more quiet conversations about the state of their constant need to find true love.

Who do I have now?

Sonia would say Rikki had the Lord. And she knew that. Rikki had certainly done her share of praying lately. The faith her mother had instilled in her had helped her through this past week.

And you have Blain.

No, she'd thought she had Blain but after all of his bluster about her being honest, he'd withheld one important thing from her. His father's career as a county sheriff.

Why? Was he as angry at his father as she wanted to be with hers?

Her cell buzzed, causing her to toss aside the book she'd been trying to read. Pushing at the bed covers, she stared at the caller ID.

Blain.

She almost threw the phone across the room but Rikki wondered if something else had happened. It was getting late so why else would he call?

She tapped the screen. "Yes?"

"I know you're angry—"

"You don't know me at all."

"Look, Rikki, it's complicated."

"I've heard that excuse before."

"We need to talk but not over the phone."

Did he think her cell was bugged?

Just the thought scared Rikki and made her angry all over again.

"I can't leave," she reminded him. "Not even to go out and get some fresh air."

"I know. And it's better if I don't come out there."

"So we can't talk to each other. That might be for the best, don't you think?"

She ended the call, which should have brought her a certain measure of satisfaction. Instead, Rikki curled up in her bed and stared at the sliver of the moon she saw caught between the scurrying clouds high up in the winter sky.

She was still all alone.

TEN

Blain stared at the phone for a few minutes.

He guessed he deserved a hang-up or two. He hadn't trusted Rikki in the beginning and now that he did trust her, now that he wanted to help her and get to know her and see her, she'd turned on him.

Or maybe she'd never trusted him from the start.

Alvanetti. She was an Alvanetti. He needed to readjust his way of thinking and stick to the facts. So instead of calling her back, he headed to the police station.

He'd talk to someone else familiar with this case.

The suspect.

By the time he got to the station, a slow cold rain had set in. A winter chill covered the night. Before he could get in out of the rain, a figure stepped out of the shadows.

"Detective, got a minute?"

Blain turned to find Santo Alvanetti standing there in an expensive-looking black wool coat.

"Can I help you, Mr. Alvanetti?" Blain asked, impatient to get to the suspect. And surprised to see Rikki's hostile brother here.

Santo's dark scowl twisted around his face. "I'd like to talk to you, yes."

"Come in," Blain said. He might be able to get inside Santo's head and see if Rikki's brother could shed some light on things. But an Alvanetti being in such close proximity to the shooter they'd captured earlier today didn't set well with Blain. Santo could be here trying to warn that man to stay quiet or else.

Blain took Santo into a small conference room and shut the door. "Would you like something to drink?"

"No." Santo took off his coat and pushed his hand through his dark hair. "I'm worried about my family."

Blain sat down. "Yes, I could tell that this morning."

Santo's scowl went even blacker. "You think I was cruel to my sister?"

"You could say that. You and your father seem to like to shift blame."

Santo leaned forward and tapped a finger on the table. "My father and I have no involvement in this. We have ways of doing our own investigations, though."

"Don't interfere with this case," Blain said. "You'll regret it."

"Don't threaten me," Santo said. "You'll regret it."

Blain leaned back and stared him down. "Why are you here?"

"I don't like that someone managed to shoot at my sister and kill one of my men." He shrugged. "Our place out on the lake has always been a haven of sorts."

"Yeah, like impenetrable."

"But someone breached it today," Santo said, his dark face etched in anger and weariness.

"Nobody likes that." Blain got out his pocket notebook. "Mind if I take notes?"

"Please do," Santo replied. "I have nothing to hide."

Blain let that go on by for now. "Do you have any ideas on who might be after Rikki?"

"Here's what I know," Santo said. "We run a legitimate business. We import antiques and estate jewelry and run a vast warehouse and online site. Someone out there must want something and they think Rikki has that something."

"But she doesn't use your services, right?"

Santo stared down at the table. "Yes and no. She uses some warehouses in Miami and Tallahassee and some of the pieces she buys could have possibly been shipped through our site."

"Does she know this?"

"No and she has no reason to know this. And I'd like to keep it that way. Rikki is stubborn and smart and proud. We can't control who orders what from us or how it ships once it's out there in various establishments and venues. But if someone smuggled something into a shipment and she received it, she could be in danger. Does that make sense?"

"Yes." Blain jotted notes. "Are you willing to let me go over your shipment records? I'd have to ask her about her clients again and also about her vendors."

Santo stood. "I don't mind helping you find this criminal. But I want it clear—our family is clean now. I have children, Detective. I'm not like my father. I just need you to know that. I won't be harassed over this."

Blain didn't plan on harassing Santo but he would question him over and over if needed. "Why were you so angry at Rikki this morning?"

"Lots going on. My brother Victor's been calling, wanting answers, too. Or at least, he called earlier today. Now I can't get him to return my calls."

"He needs to call us. We've tried to find him

and he seems to be just as elusive as the victim's missing brother."

"Victor keeps to himself," Santo said. "I told him what I knew but he was fishing for information. Probably concerned about the bank accounts."

"Should he be concerned?" Blain asked.

A blank expression dropped down across Santo's olive-skinned face. "Yes, since he hasn't contributed to the family coffers a lot."

"Are *you* worried about money?"

Santo tugged on his coat. "I'd had a bad morning and as I told you, I won't be harassed over this. I've got enough to deal with right now. My wife left me." With that, he shook Blain's hand and walked to the door. "Don't disappoint me, Detective. Our family doesn't need this right now. Make it go away."

Blain stared after Santo, resenting how the entire family managed to issue orders left and right. Santo Alvanetti seemed like a hard man to deal with, a man who could be trying to cover his own secrets. Maybe his wife had had enough, too. Had Santo taken the company to a new level—a legitimate business level? Or had he somehow put everyone he loved in danger?

If so, he could be playing the locals the way his father always had. But Blain wasn't one to get played. He tried calling Hunter Lawson again.

Hunter could dig into these types of things in a discreet way.

After leaving Hunter a message, he put his notebook away and started for the door.

His phone buzzed.

"What now?"

When he saw Rikki's number, he spun around and went back into the conference room. "Hello."

"Blain, my father's not home. He left a while ago and he's not home. One of the guards just let me know. He didn't take anyone with him and he hasn't checked in. I'm really worried."

"I'm on my way." He didn't stop to consider she could have called someone from the sheriff's office. He didn't stop to consider anything except that he needed to help Rikki.

His friends' warnings might be right.

He could be in way over his head.

Rikki wondered how much more she'd have to deal with. Where was Franco? Her father never left without a driver. He rarely drove himself anywhere. Why start now?

She'd left messages with her brother Santo, thinking maybe Papa had gone to the warehouse out near the river. But Santo wasn't answering his phone.

She paced the den in sweatpants and a big sweater. After checking on her mother and telling Peggy what was going on, she'd called Blain. Although some of the guards had gone to look for Franco, Rikki's heart told her to alert Blain since this was just too much of a coincidence after this morning.

Had the same people who were after her tried to take her father?

She heard the door swinging open and turned from the fire to find Blain hurrying up the hallway.

He stopped, his eyes meeting hers. "Hi."

"Hi." Rikki didn't think. She ran into his arms. "I'm so worried. I… I shouldn't have called you but… I trust you."

There. She'd admitted it. In spite of the chasm that seemed to stretch between them, she did trust Blain. But she had to add one other thing. "And I think my father trusts you, too."

"It's okay," he said, standing back, his hands on her elbows. "Could be nothing or it could be important, considering everything that's happened so far."

She stepped back. "That's what I was thinking. So what can we do?"

"I've alerted the sheriff's department and I've got a couple of patrols searching the roads between here and town. Did your father indicate where he might be going?"

"No. I didn't even know he'd left." She shook

her head. "We actually had a good talk this afternoon and then after he had dinner, he went back to his office. I sat with my mother for a while and then went to my room to read."

"Who's with her now?"

"Peggy, her night nurse."

"Trustworthy?"

"You had her vetted. What do you think?"

"I need to know what you think."

"Peggy is solid. She's one of the best people I know."

"Okay. Let's start in your father's office. Maybe he got a call or left some notes."

"I'll take you in there."

Blain followed her down the hall to her father's big study on the opposite side of the house from the bedroom wing. The curtains were open to a view of the boat dock and the water beyond. A lone security light shimmered in the rain.

Blain went to the glass doors centered between the windows. "Locked tight. No sign of forced entry."

"That rules out abduction," Rikki said, relief washing over her. "He could have gone to the warehouse but he would have let someone drive him."

"So we think he left on his own. Unless someone called him and forced him to leave alone."

Her heart hit hard again, ramping up her pulse.

"I'm afraid he was involved in an accident." She started searching her father's desk. "Blain, what if…if he's hurt or worse?"

"Hey, we'll figure it out," he said, coming to help her. "I'll talk to the guards and see if they know what time he left."

"It had to have been after eight," she said, her hand going over the stack of papers near the phone. "But it's past ten now and he's usually in bed around nine thirty. I checked his room next to my mother's. His bed is still made."

"Let's keep looking," Blain said.

Rikki lifted invoices and antique magazines, a stack of opened mail and several Christmas cards.

Then she saw a scribbled note that contained one word. *Victor.*

"Your brother?"

Rikki nodded, noticing Blain's interest. "He rarely calls. He's been in Europe for years and… he and my father are not close anymore."

"Do you think he called your father?"

"Maybe. We've been trying to let him know about mother's condition." She kept glancing over the papers. "If Victor called, he could be in trouble or he could have run out of money. He hasn't bothered to call and check on our mother very often, either." Victor wasn't the worrying type unless it involved him.

"I'll see what else I can find out about Victor's whereabouts," Blain said. "Meantime, I'll check with the guards and then I'm going out to search for your father myself."

"I'm going with you," Rikki said. At his disapproving look, she added, "I can't sit here worrying, Blain."

"This could be another bad idea," Blain said as they hurried out of the house. "Why don't you listen to me and stay here?"

"I'm too upset," Rikki said. "If you don't let me go with you I'll make one of the men take me or I'll go by myself."

"Get in the car," Blain said, his mind absorbing this latest turn of events. He'd have to watch her or she'd bolt. He'd talked to two guards and they both agreed it wasn't like Franco to just leave on his own.

"The old man's been acting strange for a few weeks now," one of the burly men told Blain. "He's always on the phone or mumbling to himself. He's a mess over Miss Sonia being so sick."

The other guard had nodded. "And now his only daughter being attacked. Something's up. Things are just weird around here."

Blain agreed with that understatement. He had to consider the Alvanetti family could be in some kind of turf war with another group.

Santo had come to see him and mentioned Victor had been calling. Could their brother be involved with some sort of smuggling ring?

Blain didn't have the resources to search the entire state for competitors but he might have to do just that. He'd put in another call to Hunter Lawson but he had yet to hear from the Okie. The private detective would be an asset right about now.

Once they were on the road, he laid down some ground rules. "You have to do what I say, Rikki. If I stop this vehicle to search along the way, I need you to stay with me. Okay?"

"Okay."

"Or stay in the car."

"Okay. But… I don't want to stay in the car."

Blain let out a sigh. "You are one of the most stubborn women I've ever met."

"I'm assertive, not stubborn. Where are you going?"

"To the Alvanetti Shipping Warehouse first. You said your father might have gone there."

"Possibly." She stared out into the night. "But it's not like him to go out at night without a driver. His eyes aren't all that good from what I can tell."

Blain wanted to ask her more but she'd only been back around Franco for a week now. Did she really know anything more about her family than he did?

When they reached the warehouse, Rikki shouted and pointed. "There's his car."

Blain breathed a sigh of relief, but this wasn't over yet. "The whole place is dark," he said. "I'm calling for backup just in case."

"Good idea." She didn't wait for him but got out of the car and started toward the front office doors.

Blain barely managed to catch her. "Rikki, stop. Think, okay? We have to approach with caution."

She nodded. "I'm sorry."

He called for help and then pulled her close. "Stay behind me or I'll lock you in the back of the car, understand?"

"Yes."

Blain touched a hand to her hair. "And you should have worn a coat."

"Let's go," she said.

Blain tugged her to the car while he pulled out a flashlight. "No lights on. That can't be good."

"We might not be able to get inside," she whispered. "I can call my brother Santo."

"Let's look first." Blain had Santo's number but he'd have to explain to her why. And he couldn't do that right now.

They made it to the door and Blain checked around it. "Has to be an alarm system."

"Yes. There's a lot of valuable stuff in this warehouse." Rikki grabbed his arm. "Do you think there's something here that would cause someone to kill?" She shook her head. "I don't want my family to be involved. I couldn't handle that."

Blain didn't want to admit it, but he'd thought long and hard about her family being involved. It made sense, after all.

"Anything is plausible at this point."

He touched a hand to the glass-paneled double doors and pushed. One of the doors swung open.

"That's not good, either," Rikki said. "Blain, this is dangerous."

Blain held her behind him. "Which is why we're going to wait here for backup."

He didn't want her to see in case something bad had happened to her father. She might resent her family's reputed criminal activity and she might not be close to Franco but he could tell Rikki loved her family in spite of everything.

A good reminder that he still had to handle this case with kid gloves.

Because blood was always thicker than murder, after all.

ELEVEN

Two cruisers and a sheriff's-department SUV showed up in record time. When the Alvanetti warehouse was messed with, everyone came running.

"Whadda we got?" The sheriff's deputy asked, his gun and flashlight out.

Blain knew the young deputy. "Hey, Billy. Not sure yet," Blain said after the two Millbrook officers hurried up. "Franco Alvanetti is missing so we decided to check here, since according to his daughter, Regina, he sometimes comes here late to work." He indicated Rikki behind him. "We got here and found the door unlocked."

"He'd lock the door behind him," Rikki said. "His car is parked over there." She pointed to a big oak tree off to the side of the building.

"I'll go check the vehicle," one of the officers said, hurrying away.

"Let's get in there," Blain said. "Rikki, you

stay behind me, okay?" He couldn't leave her in the car so he had to let her go in.

She nodded but her eyes held a solid apprehension. She grabbed Blain's jacket and held tight.

Soon they were moving through the dark front offices. Blain noticed opulent furnishings and several cubicles and conference rooms. They passed what looked like a kitchen and dining area.

"Where's the main office?" he asked. "Where would he go?"

She pointed to the left. "The one in the corner with the river view."

Blain saw the big windows and the glistening Millbrook River beyond the security lights and the mushrooming trees. The cloudy night didn't allow for much light to creep in so he held his flashlight over his weapon.

"There!" Rikki pointed behind the big desk. "It's him."

Blain rushed over and found Franco lying on the floor. He checked Franco's pulse. "He's alive." Then he shouted, "Call 911 and get an ambulance out here. And someone go over the rest of this place and check for any sign of intruders."

Everyone scrambled into action. Rikki fell on her knees beside Franco. "Papa? Papa, wake up." She touched his forehead and took one of his beefy hands in hers. "Daddy?"

Blain turned on the office light and pulled her away. "Let me check him out, okay?"

She nodded, her expression void of emotion. She looked as if all the blood had left her body. "I need to call Santo," she said, her voice above a whisper.

"I can do that," Blain said, his hands moving over Franco's body. When he touched the older man's head, his fingers came away with blood. "He's got a bad gash on the back of his head."

Rikki took in a shattered breath. "Someone hit him?"

"Or he fell and hit his head."

Blain grabbed Franco's overcoat from the desk chair and placed it around him. Then he checked the older man's vitals again. Weak, shaky pulse but no other obvious signs of injury. The paramedic would have to determine the rest. "Help is on the way, Rikki, okay?"

She bobbed her head. "He looks so old, Blain. When did he get so old?"

Blain held one hand to her father's erratic pulse and then took her hand. "Hang on. Both of you need to hang on."

A month ago, Franco Alvanetti had only come to mind whenever Blain thought of bringing the reputed crime boss down. That and how he resented his own father for turning a blind eye. Now his whole perspective was changing. The

Alvanetti family was more complicated than he'd ever imagined.

Starting with the woman kneeling by her father with her eyes closed in prayer.

Sirens echoed out over the night. Rikki got up to run to the door. "They're here."

"And we need to stand back and let them to their jobs," Blain said.

He did a quick visual of the entire room and saw a small white statue lying by the ornate credenza. He quickly snapped a picture of the statue, sure that someone had used it to hit Franco over the head. Then he dug into his jacket pocket and found a pair of latex gloves. After putting them on, he picked up the statue. It was a goddess of some sort, heavy white porcelain. A big jagged crack indicated it had been chipped on one corner. A dark stain spread against the damaged part.

Blood?

Rikki saw his actions and gasped. "That's one of his favorite pieces. My mother bought it in Italy and teased him that the face looked like hers. He loves it." She walked to the credenza. "He kept it right here."

Blain saw bloodstains on the base of the foot-high figurine. Someone had definitely used this as a weapon.

One of the other officers hurried into the office. "Sir, we found something else." He gave Blain a pointed stare.

Rikki didn't miss a beat. "Just tell him."

Blain nodded at the officer. "Go ahead."

"We found a body," the young man said. "Out back by a Dumpster."

Rikki put a hand to her mouth. "Is it my brother?"

The man shook his head. "No, ma'am." Then he walked over to Blain and whispered, "It looks like the picture we have up at the station. The one of Chad Presley."

Blain's gaze locked with Rikki's.

"What is it?" she asked, her hand grabbing the sleeve of Blain's jacket. "Blain?"

He couldn't hide it from her. "It might be Chad, Rikki. I'm sorry."

Rikki's eyes turned a misty black. "Show me."

When he didn't move, she gripped his sleeve again. "Blain, let me see him."

Blain nodded and turned to the other officer. "Bag and tag this, Wilson."

Then he and Rikki headed out to the back of the property where a group of officers were gathered. They parted when Blain brought Rikki toward the grim scene.

She pushed past him, but he held her back, his hands on her arms. "Rikki, is this Chad Presley?"

She stood so still he was afraid he'd lost her.

Finally, she bobbed her head. "Yes, that's him. That's Chad."

Blain turned her around. She was shaking. "Somebody get me a blanket for Miss Alvanetti, please."

It looked like the killer was now targeting the entire Alvanetti family and people connected with them. And it was obvious whoever was doing this wanted something very important.

Blain was more determined than ever to find out what exactly that might be.

Rikki sat at the hospital with her brother Santo, both staring at a kitschy watercolor on the waiting room wall. Caught in a grip of horror over what had happened tonight, her mind moved from finding Tessa dead to seeing her father lying so still…and then seeing a man she'd been close to for years sitting up against a Dumpster with blood all over his clothes.

And now, her brother staring off into space, his expression full of anger and what looked like his own private despair.

Santo had been furious, of course. He'd ranted at Blain and her and the police and the paramedics. Now he sat with a brooding frown, his hands in the pockets of his winter coat.

"I can get us some coffee," she offered, thinking her brothers and her had never been close.

But she was rethinking that and a lot of other things these days.

Santo burrowed deeper into his coat. "I don't need any coffee."

Rikki glanced at the ER doors. They'd been in there with her father a long time. Blain had left a few minutes ago to take the bagged figurine to the station to log as evidence and to talk to the medical examiner about Chad's body. Thinking she'd never sleep again, she glanced at her brother.

"They didn't find anything missing," she said, needing to talk about this. "Nothing, even though the office was a mess. The warehouse looked intact."

"I heard that but I've got some of my staff walking it right now along with some officers to see if anything else is messed up. I intend to go over the inventory again first thing in the morning. A professional would cover his tracks."

She stood and whirled to stare at her brother. "What have I done, Santo? What is it about me that this family can't love?"

Santo pulled a hand through his thick black hair. He looked as exhausted as she felt. "What is it about this family that *you* can't love, *mia sorella*?"

That question floored Rikki. "Isn't that obvious? We live dangerous lives, lives of secrets and sins. I had to get away but our lifestyle has finally caught up with us."

Santo looked shocked and sickened. "You judge too harshly, Regina."

"I know what I see."

His dark eyes scanned her with regret. "You know what you think you see." Staring ahead, he said, "Two people you met after you left here are dead. What does that tell you?"

"You're cruel," she replied, gritting her teeth at the pain coursing through her. But he was right.

"I'm realistic," he retorted. "You always did only see what your so-called noble heart needed to see and nothing else."

"I see that someone is after me and now my family." She tugged her sweater close. "And I'm beginning to wonder if my family isn't involved in something none of us can control."

"What do you care?" he asked, rage radiating from his eyes. "You and Victor, you both chose to leave me with this mess."

"What do you mean?"

Santo gave her a long, measuring stare. "I…"

The ER doors swung open then, causing him to stand and turn toward the doctor coming up the hallway.

Rikki watched her brother's face, sure that Santo knew something he wasn't telling her, but then that had been the pattern with her family for most of her life. But she'd have to wait to find out. The doctor didn't look as though he had good news.

Blain finished filing his report and pushed back his squeaking desk chair. He planned to head back to the hospital to check on Mr. Alvanetti and Rikki. Her brother was with her and Santo had brought his own guards with him, right along with his own uncooperative attitude.

But Blain worried, anyway. The neighborhood canvas back at the townhome hadn't brought any answers. A couple of joggers had been spotted that afternoon but the descriptions were vague and could fit anyone. Blain had been jogging there himself so he couldn't dispute the statements.

No prints anywhere. Nothing yet on the brother in Europe.

No solid evidence on any of her clients being involved. The all had alibis and clean records.

Now a shooting attempt this morning and an attack at the warehouse and a dead ex-boyfriend. Franco was in the hospital and Chad Presley was dead. He had to wonder again what the ex-boyfriend's involvement in this could have been. Chad had somehow made his way west from Tallahassee to the panhandle, maybe looking for Rikki or maybe looking for something else. They'd never get a chance to interview Presley now. But Blain did have something to add to his notes.

He remembered Rikki telling him Chad had been at a wedding at the estate last spring. Had he scoped the place, searching for something? Maybe gone to the warehouse and confronted the old man? But then, who had killed Chad and why?

The crime scene people had determined that the slug they'd found embedded in the fence behind Chad Presley had matched the one they'd found near Tessa Jones's body. Possibly the same shooter.

His phone buzzed. Lawson. Finally.

"Hey," he said. "Thanks for calling me back."

"What you got?" Hunter asked. Not one for small talk.

"It's a long story," Blain said. He gave Hunter the particulars. "I need you to do some digging, especially in the state capital and maybe down in Miami. Are you nearby? Can you take this on?"

"Not nearby but I'll be there soon enough," Hunter replied. "Email me the facts."

"I'll get right on that," Blain said.

He hung up, relief washing over him. Now if he could just get a hit on Victor Alvanetti.

Blain didn't have a lot of resources and he had

no European connections. He stared at his notes and then lifted his head.

But he knew someone who did.

Time to make this investigation a family affair.

He grabbed his coat and headed back out into the night.

When he got to the hospital, he found Rikki and Santo huddled together in a corner. Rikki glanced up and saw him and then shot out of her chair after giving her scowling brother a worried look.

"Hi," she said, meeting Blain near another hallway.

"Hi. What's the status?"

"He has a concussion," she said. "He's okay but while they were examining him his blood pressure spiked." She pushed at her tousled hair and looked over her shoulder. "They want to keep him here to rest for the night and…they want to do some more tests in the morning. The doctor said my father is suffering from exhaustion, too."

"Exhaustion?" That shocked Blain. "I thought he was retired and kind of hanging out at the house most days."

"I thought that, too," she said with a lift of her shoulders. "I think he stays up half the night, sitting with my mother even though she has a nurse."

"That's understandable," Blain said. "In spite of everything, they seem to love each other."

He looked into Rikki's chocolate eyes and wondered what that kind of love would be like. Would he ever know? Up until now, he hadn't really expected a lasting relationship with a woman. But there was something about her. Those pretty, pink lips, those exotic, slanted eyes and dark, winged eyebrows.

"Did you find anything?"

Blain tore his gaze away from Rikki to find her brother staring him down from behind her with a dark, threatening scowl.

"Uh, no. No viable witnesses have come forward about seeing anyone entering or leaving the town house the other night and our shooter from this morning apparently has lost his will to speak. And nothing regarding tonight at the warehouse. We'll go over the security tapes and maybe that will help us identify your father's assailant since he's indicated he didn't see who attacked him." He held back and then said, "And we need to find Chad's killer."

He didn't mention the ballistics report.

"The door was open," Rikki reminded Santo. "Could you have left it unlocked?"

Her brother stepped back, his scowl widening. "No, I didn't leave it unlocked. Papa probably unlocked it and forgot to lock it back. He's been forgetful lately."

"That's a possibility," Blain said, seeing the concern flaring in Rikki's eyes. "We don't know whether it happened before or after Presley was killed, but someone entered after your dad and hit him over the head."

"And if he knew that person, that makes it all the worse that it happened," Rikki said. "I have no idea what Chad was doing there."

"Did he know your father?" Blain asked.

"No. I didn't introduce Chad to my father at the wedding that day."

Santo turned away, disgust shadowing his features. "It's bad that this happened, no matter who did it."

Blain noticed the brother's agitated state. Worry about his father, or worry about being exposed?

"I need to ask both of you a favor," he said, following Santo back to the quiet corner.

Rikki sat down by her brother. "What is it?"

Blain sank on a chair across from them. "I need to question Victor, too. But I don't have the resources or the funds to search in Europe."

"And that involves us how?" Santo asked, his

frown creasing like a row of sand dunes. He started fidgeting and stared at the floor.

Blain didn't flinch. "I need your help. You know people over there, including your brother, Victor. He's been calling so now's the time to question him."

"We haven't heard from Victor in months," Rikki said. "Not since Mama got so ill while she was visiting him in Italy."

Santo looked down at the floor. "He's been calling me, KK. And Papa, too. But he's stopped since…since all of this started."

Rikki narrowed her eyes at her brother. "I found Victor's name in Papa's office. Why didn't you mention this?"

"I figured he wanted money," Santo said. "He claimed he'd heard things and that he was concerned but we both know that's not true."

Blain made a note of that. "He could help us."

"He doesn't care," Santo retorted. "Victor is all about Victor, after all."

Reminding himself that nothing was as it seemed with this family, Blain took a slow breath. "Do you think you can help me find Victor?" he asked Santo.

Rikki shot Santo an imploring glance. "Yes, we can. I don't want anyone coming after my family again. I want this over with. Two attacks and two murders in one day are more than enough for me. We lost a guard and… Chad is dead. We could have lost Papa, too."

Blain nodded and then glanced over at Santo and waited for him to speak up.

When he didn't, Rikki continued. "We'll do whatever needs to be done to end this, of course."

Santo continued to stare down at the fake wooden floor, his dark eyes as stormy as the night. "We might not be able to locate Victor."

Blain leaned forward. "You came to see me earlier tonight, Santo. You said you'd help me because you're concerned about your family. Locating and questioning your brother will go a long way toward that end."

Rikki pivoted toward her brother. "You talked to Blain?"

"I did," Santo said. "I want to keep *my* family out of this."

"Too late," Blain said. "I'm beginning to think you're all involved."

Santo shook his head. "We just need to find out what is going on so we can prove we're not."

"I agree," Rikki said. "I'm worried about Victor, too. He could be in danger, too."

"We're all in danger," Santo said on a growl. Then he got up and looked at his watch. "I have to go home and pay the babysitter and send her home. I'll check back in the morning."

Rikki looked surprised. "Where is Althea?"

Santo shook out his coat. "My wife left for Miami this morning. And I don't think she'll be returning anytime soon. We are officially separated."

TWELVE

After her brother left, Rikki sat staring out the waiting room window.

The night was dark and full of thunder and lightning. A persistent wind lifted the red bows tied around the huge posts supporting the ER portico. She shivered and felt a hand on her arm. Then a warm leather coat over her shoulders.

Blain's hand. Blain's coat.

"You don't have to stay," she said. "I have guards all around me."

He sat down beside her. "I'm taking you home. You can't see your father again until tomorrow, anyway, so you need to get some rest."

Feeling torn, she tugged the big jacket closer around her shoulders. The smell of old leather and spicy aftershave assaulted her with an overwhelming, endearing need. She was thankful for Blain at that moment, thankful that God had sent her a strong protector.

She could live right here in this warm cocoon

that shouted Blain. But she needed to check on her mother. And she needed to know that no one would hurt her father. That realization left her surprised and off-kilter.

"What do I do, Blain?" she asked, surrendering to the need to let someone else help her for a change. "What do I do? My friend is dead, my ex-boyfriend is dead, and my family is at risk. My brother who never confides in me is obviously going through some sort of crisis in his marriage. I've been so out of touch and now that I'm back, everything is falling apart."

"Maybe things were already falling apart before you got here."

She hadn't considered that. Had Tessa's murder just been part of something bigger and even more sinister? "I don't know whom to believe."

He lifted her up, his hands on her elbows. "I don't have all the answers, but right now you're coming with me."

Rikki glanced at the nurses' station. "I should check—"

"He's stable," Blain said. "And we have a man at his door."

"Okay." She gave in and allowed him to guide her out the double doors and into the parking lot. A lone, fake Christmas tree in the center of a tiny park sparkled with brightly colored lights. Rikki had to keep reminding herself that this was supposed to be a season of love and peace but she expected something terrible around every corner. Too many shadows overpowered the bright lights. But she knew God was in control, no matter how she tried to fix things.

Blain held her in the crook of his arm, his gaze moving all around the nearly empty hospital parking lot. When they got to his vehicle, she noticed he was driving a big truck tonight. He opened the passenger-side door and helped her up but the truck was high and she was too short to make the step.

Blain lifted her without even a grunt and placed her on the seat. When their eyes met, a soothing warmth flooded her entire system like a warm ocean current. His midnight eyes moved over her face to settle on her lips. He held her there, his gaze washing her in a longing that only mirrored the one in her heart.

Rikki wondered why this man made her feel so different, so safe and secure, so important. She wanted to say a lot of things to him but she held back.

He's a cop, she reminded herself. If Blain found out her family was involved in Tessa's murder and everything else that had happened, he'd never forgive her.

And he'd walk away from her forever.

So she touched a hand to his face and turned on the seat, his jacket still covering her.

Blain's eyes stayed on her but he made sure she was in and then he shut the door and came around the truck and got inside.

"I'm not taking you home right away," he said.

"Why not?"

"You need a break."

"I need to check on my mother."

"Call and talk to Peggy."

"Blain…"

"Just an hour, Rikki. An hour away from all of this. I'll get you home soon enough."

What could she say? She wanted an hour away. Since she'd been home, her life had become a whirlwind of trying to stay one step ahead of a killer. She'd ignored her clients and she'd ignored her friends. She'd tried to ignore the way her heart beat a little faster each time this man came near her.

But she couldn't ignore the way Blain made her feel. Not any longer, not tonight when her world seemed to be careening out of control.

So she said a prayer, asking God to help her fight at this enemy so she could protect her family. It no longer mattered what they'd done in the past. She could forgive that and she would somehow *have to* forgive that. She asked for a blanket of protection and she prayed God would give them all the answers to save them.

And then she tugged Blain's coat around her and nodded.

"An hour would be nice."

Blain maneuvered the pickup up underneath the camp house pilings so the house would help hide the vehicle. He'd never brought a woman out to the camp house before. None of them had at first.

But he knew Alec had brought his fiancée, Marla, out here once to give her a break from her troubles so he figured it might work for Rikki, too. He accepted that bringing her here meant he had crossed the line from protector to something more personal. He wasn't quite sure what that something was but Blain knew he needed this hour away, too.

"What place is this?" Rikki asked as he helped her out of the truck.

He heard the wariness in her words. "Just an old beach cottage my friends and I bought together. We use it for fishing and hunting and downtime."

She smiled and inhaled the cold night air. "A good idea. You and your friends seem close."

Blain guided her around the truck and up the planked steps to the big screen porch on the bay side of the house. "We are. We all met after coming back here to Millbrook, over a serious dart game at the pizza house. After we compared notes, we realized we'd all been in the military. Alec Caldwell was a captain in the marines."

"I know him," she said, surprise coloring her words. "He's on the client list I gave you."

Blain nodded. "Yeah, I talked to him. He gave you a glowing report by the way."

"That's good to know."

Blain opened the door to the house and went straight to the fireplace. "I'll get it warm in here."

He motioned to a sofa in front of the fire. "Have a seat."

She settled on the old leather couch and glanced around.

Deciding small talk would calm her, Blain went about getting the fire started. "Then there's Preacher—Rory Sanderson. He was an army chaplain and now he's the pastor at Millbrook Lake Church. He'll be officiating Alec and Marla's wedding right before Christmas."

"Oh, the wedding." She shook out her hair. "I so wanted to attend but now…"

"We can make that happen if you really want to go."

"I don't want to put anyone in any danger. Especially not at a wedding."

Blain wouldn't be able to watch out for her since he had best-man duties. "Maybe you'll be safe again by then."

She leaned back on the sofa and grabbed a fleece throw and dragged it up over her lap. "I don't know if I'll ever feel safe again."

Satisfied with the fire, Blain walked over and sat down beside her. "You can, for now at least. Sit back and relax for a few minutes."

She smiled over at him and then pointed toward the big window in the dining nook. "Nice Christmas tree."

Blain twisted around. "Preacher. He loves Christmas." He got up and plugged in the pathetic little tree. "He also sees the beauty in what most of us would deem unsalvageable."

"It is beautiful," she said, her voice soft and quiet.

Blain came back to her and looked at the tiny white twinkling lights on the scrawny little cedar tree. Then he turned to Rikki. "I guess it is, at that."

She was crying.

The real kind of crying that every man on earth dreaded.

But these silent, quiet sobs weren't about the little Christmas tree. She'd held them tight since the night she'd found her friend dead and now, the trauma of today and finding her father passed out with a gash to his head and a man she'd dated dead, had caused the letdown of emotions she'd tried so hard to hold back. And that letdown had turned into a deluge of pain and anger and grief.

Blain didn't think. He just pulled her into his arms and held her there, his hands working to pull the blanket up over her shivering body.

She turned and laid her head against his chest and then she snuggled close to him. She felt so fragile and tiny there in his embrace but she also fit perfectly. Blain had to swallow back the emotions clogging his throat. What was happening between them?

He couldn't explain it, so he held her there and watched the fire while the little Christmas tree's lights flashed off and on. Soon, Rikki's sobs turned into soft, steady breaths.

She'd fallen asleep.

Rikki's dreams changed from running in terror out in the cold to being anchored in warm and love. She could see her house, the big house where she'd grown up, off in the distance.

Then she saw her husband, Drake, waving to her from a shore that she couldn't reach. She cried out to him but he turned and walked away. Rikki looked around, searching for help. She saw a rustic square house set up on big pilings. A small Christmas tree shone inside the window.

She ran toward that house.

And then she woke up and met a solid chest. Blain's chest.

She glanced up to find him staring at her, memories of her meltdown coming back into focus.

"Has it been an hour?" she asked, still disoriented, her eyes burning.

He checked his watch. "You have five minutes to spare."

Rikki didn't want to move. And she didn't want to tear her eyes away from Blain.

"Five minutes," he whispered. "Just enough time for this."

Then he lowered his mouth to hers and kissed her with such a sweet tenderness that she almost started crying again. Or maybe she was still dreaming. Maybe she'd kept running toward that little house and now she was with this man in that same dream.

But the pressure of his lips on hers was no dream.

It was a sweet reality that touched her and scared her and made her want to run away again.

But she was so tired of running. Turning in his arms, Rikki welcomed Blain's kiss. How had she become so thirsty? So alone and parched and wanting? Being here with Blain felt as if she'd come out of a dark wilderness. He felt like an answered prayer.

And yet they had so much between them still.

Pulling away, Rikki sat up. "I'm so sorry. I… I shouldn't have let that happen."

"*I* let it happen," he said, his eyes washed in a black regret. "I let it happen, Rikki."

She moved away, the blanket now suddenly cloying. "Did you want it to happen?"

"No. Yes. Never. Only since the minute I first saw you."

She could almost state feeling the same. "But murder is a buzzkill, right?"

"Yep." He checked his watch. "We need to go."

"After that kiss? That's all you have to say?"

Blain stood and went to stoke the fire. A symbolic move if ever there was one. "What can I say? I'd like to kiss you again but we both know how this works."

She started folding the blanket, her need to spar with him back and intact. "Why did you bring me here?"

"To give you some time to relax. Maybe to… grieve."

Embarrassed, she shook her head. "Well, I've done both and more."

He unplugged the tree's lights and walked back over to her. "Hey, so let's not get all bent out of shape now that our hour of quiet is over." When she refused to look at him, he lifted her chin with one finger. "Rikki, we both know what we're facing here. Your family has a history—"

"I know," she said. "I know better than anyone."

"And I understand, better than anyone. My dad let things slide but I'm not my dad."

"And I'm not my father," she retorted, drained of any feelings now. "This brought us together but I won't let it tear us apart. I need you to find that killer. After that, the rest is up to you." She started for the door.

Blain grabbed her arm and tugged her around. "Hey, nothing is going to tear us apart."

"But you still have doubts about me, don't you?"

"Not about you," Blain said. "About your family, yes."

"And there it is. How can you kiss me and then tell me that?"

"I'm attracted to you," he replied. "But I have to do my job."

She nodded, the warm cocoon torn beyond repair. "Well, right now your job is to get me home to my mother."

"Let's go." He checked the house and walked with her out onto the porch. Then he said, "I know what you're doing, Rikki."

She doubted he knew anything about her. "Oh, and what is that?"

"You're deflecting what you're feeling right back onto me."

"And what exactly am I feeling?"

"You loved another man once and I don't think you're over him yet. Or maybe you're afraid something will happen to me in the same way. Right?"

Rikki's heart did a tumble. Realization curled around her like a finger of fog over the water. She'd pushed so many men away since she'd lost Drake. But Blain? She didn't want to push him away. She wanted to be back in his arms, safe and secure.

Only she couldn't admit that yet. Not now. Not when her life was in so much chaos. And not when Blain's own life could be on the line, too.

"I'm afraid of a lot of things," she finally said. Then she turned to face him. "Thank you for bringing me here. It did help to let go and get some of this out of my system."

She saw how the implication of her words had hit him. His eyes held a trace of hurt along with that regret she'd seen earlier. So he took her down to the truck and got her inside without a word.

Rikki took one last look at the little house on the bay. And she knew she'd never forget the one hour she'd spent there with Blain. A good cry and a good kiss.

It would have to be enough for now.

THIRTEEN

They were on the bay road when Blain noticed a car tailing them. He didn't say anything to Rikki but he watched the headlights dip and sway as they moved closer. This road wasn't heavily traveled, especially this late at night.

Five miles till they reached the Alvanetti estate.

He did not need another thing to happen today but it was early morning so technically it was tomorrow. The pursuers apparently didn't want to quit anytime soon. When the car behind them edged up behind his truck, he at least was relieved they hadn't been assaulted at the beach house.

Stupid, to take her there in the first place.

But he'd never forget their time there.

When he glanced in the rearview mirror again, she turned and looked over her shoulder. "Are we being followed?"

He knew better than to try and shield her. "I believe so."

She sat straight up. "I'm really getting tired of this."

"Me, too."

"They must be watching my every move."

"Or they have someone reporting back to them."

She sent him a sharp stare at that comment but she didn't dispute his reasoning.

When the vehicle sped up and came a little too close for comfort, Blain had to decide if he should turn around and head back to town or get her inside the estate's gates as quickly as possible.

The automobile behind them was a dark sedan. The big car edged up to Blain's truck again. And this time, he felt the shudder of a bumper hitting chrome. "They're all in now."

Rikki held onto the dash and glanced back. "I know a back way onto the property," she said, a new determination sounding in her words.

"A back way?" That was a surprise. "Really now? Maybe these people know that same back way and maybe they've been coming and going whenever they please." He studied the car behind them. "They haven't shot at us yet. I'm thinking they want me to stop and hand you over to them."

She bobbed her head. "They're looking for something and they didn't find it at the warehouse."

The vehicle advanced and nudged at the truck. With the wet roads and sheer drop-offs to the bay on the right, Blain didn't want to play chicken. "Tell me about the back way."

She checked the rearview mirror on her side. "Not many people know about that road. It's practically buried in palmetto bushes and scrub oaks."

"And how do you know about it?"

"I found it when I used to go horseback riding. I used it to sneak in and out so the guards wouldn't follow me."

He could see her doing that. Reckless, rebellious and stubborn. Good traits at times and bad ones at other times.

"How do we get there from here?"

Rikki glanced back and then at the road ahead. "They'll try to run us off the road before we reach the gate to my house," she said. "Probably on the curve since it juts out over the bay."

"You're too good at figuring this stuff out," he retorted. But she was right. "But if they want you alive, they might try to pull up and send us off into the bramble on the other side of the road. What do *you* suggest?"

"The hidden road is past the gates. If we speed

up now, we can lose them on the curve and then turn off on the old road."

Blain stared into the mirror. "Okay. Hold on."

She gave him another gritty glance. "Got it."

Blain gunned it and headed toward the curve. If he lost control, they could go over the edge. If that car caught up and happened to nudge the truck just a little bit, they could crash and flip right off into the water below. But he couldn't let whoever was chasing them make it through the gates of the estate and he sure wasn't going to get himself or Rikki killed.

So he held tight and watched the upcoming curve. He knew the curve so he thought he could swing into it and make it through as long as no other cars were nearby.

The vehicle following them moved closer.

"They're speeding up again," Rikki said.

"I see that."

Blain pushed on the gas pedal and watched the dark, narrow road ahead. "Give me a hint about this private road. What should I look for?"

Rikki checked the passenger-side mirror. "A palm tree that juts out over the road on the left side about a quarter of a mile past the gate. When you see the tree, you need to hit the brakes and turn left about ten feet past the tree."

"Sure, I can do that while I'm trying to outrun these bozos and while I'm trying to keep us out of the bay."

She narrowed her eyes at him. "I thought you could."

He watched the headlights behind them. The other driver was advancing at a reckless speed. Maybe their pursuers did want both of them dead. "Rikki, this could get ugly. Hang on."

She didn't respond but she reached up for the grab-bar over the door. Blain could see the resolve in her expression.

They might be headed around a dangerous curve but he decided Rikki had also taken up a new direction. She wasn't going to back down anymore.

And that scared him about as much as the treacherous odds they were about to face.

Rikki watched the dark rain-slick road. She'd have to make sure she had the right palm tree and that she could warn Blain to turn left once they got past the tree.

What if the terrain had changed? What if the palm tree had been cut down? A thousand terrors rushed through her system but when she saw the curve coming up, she knew Blain would handle this. He was that kind of man. He'd take them through the woods if he had to.

"Okay, we're approaching the curve," he said.

"When we lose their headlights we have about ten seconds to get off this road."

"I'll keep watch while you drive."

He gunned it again and she felt the tug of the truck as it hugged the road and hovered near the steep drop-off into the bay. This part of Florida was hilly at times and flat at other times. This road followed a long bluff where houses were built into the countryside and looked as if they were clinging to the hills over the water. Santo had a home not far from here, but her father had built on the other side of the bay, which was more leveled out down toward the water.

"Blain, I don't see them anymore. Look for the palm tree."

"Okay." He kept his foot on the gas as they headed into the sharp turn in the road.

When the truck fishtailed, Rikki took in a deep breath and stared out at the dark water about twenty or so feet below the overgrowth. Blain let off the gas and straightened the truck but not before they skidded again.

"The tree," she said as she caught the bent trunk of the ancient shaggy palm. "Now, Blain!"

They were almost there.

She glanced back just as he swerved the truck to the left and into the overgrown bushes and bramble. Headlights!

"They're coming," she shouted.

Blain held the wheel as the truck hit the dirt and bounced, the heavy tires skidding and grinding in the mud. "Are you sure this is a road?" he said over the roar of the big engine and the truck plowing into the bramble.

"It used to be. The guards probably still use it sometimes to come and go." Her head hit the top of the truck. Wincing, she held to the grab-bar.

Blain leveled the truck and slowed down. "I think we're on some sort of lane," he called out. "Where are they?"

Rikki turned in the seat as he slowed the truck. "I don't see anything."

Blain did a one-eighty spin on the old overgrown road and turned off the truck's headlights. "Rikki, I need you to stay here while I go up to the road."

"What for?"

"I want to make sure they're not out there waiting."

"Shouldn't you call for backup?"

"Yes, but I don't have time. And if you stay with the truck you can go for help if I don't come back."

She bobbed her head and watched as he got out of the truck and hurried into the darkness. She didn't like that request. She wanted him to come back. Did she stay here or should she go after him?

Then she heard an engine roaring and what sounded like tires spinning. The other car must have tried to make the turn. Blain could be walking straight into a trap.

Rikki waited as the minutes seemed like hours and then she decided to get out and look for a weapon. She'd just put a booted foot down on a clump of dried vines when she heard a gunshot followed by running footsteps.

Where was Blain?

She stood at the back of the truck, crouched low, her breath caught against her rib cage. Afraid to move, she wished she'd gone with him. She could make it home from here but she wasn't going anywhere without Blain.

She lifted up to search for a limb or a rock. Maybe something in the back of the truck. When she spotted a tire iron in the truck bed, she grabbed it.

But before she could make a move toward the direction Blain had gone, someone grabbed her from behind and a strong hand went over her mouth. Rikki squirmed and kicked, the tire iron still in one hand.

"Shhh. It's me."

Blain.

She relaxed against him. "You scared me!"

"I told you to stay in the truck."

She whirled to face him and watched as he

put away his gun. "I was worried. I heard a car and then a gunshot."

"Yeah, they were up on the road trying to turn in here. I fired at them and they backed up and spun out."

"Did they get away?"

"Yep, but not before I got a good look at the driver and saw a partial on the license plate. There was someone in the passenger side, too."

"Did you call for help?"

"No," he said, his tone grim. "I recognized one of them, Rikki. He works for the sheriff's department."

Shock shot through her. "A police officer?"

He nodded. "A rookie deputy. He was at the warehouse earlier tonight."

"What do we do now?"

He stared out into the darkness. "We aren't going to tell anyone about this. I don't think he knows I saw his face but he has to be worried right about now. If I don't turn him in, whoever sent him will certainly read him the riot act."

"So this explains how they've been able to come after me no matter what we've tried to do."

"Yep." He did a quick glance around the woods and then opened the truck door. "And that also means that this particular officer is probably on someone's payroll."

"Someone besides the local sheriff's office," she added.

They got back in the truck and she showed him how to get her home. But they didn't talk. What was there to say? Rikki hoped her father wasn't the one calling the shots. How could he be if he'd been assaulted, too?

Or had that been a setup? Had someone mistaken him for someone else?

When they pulled up to the house, the guards came running with drawn guns. They must have heard the gunshots. Rikki got out and waved them away. "I'm okay."

The burly men backed off but stayed nearby.

"I can see why you wanted to get away from here," Blain said. "No privacy and shady characters everywhere." He walked her to the door. "I hate to leave you."

Rikki's heart clutched at that comment but the assumption that this place was still corrupt brought her back to reality. "I'll be all right. I just want a shower and sleep."

He nodded then stared down at her, his eyes colored with a new urgency. "Do you trust all of these people who help out around here?"

She nodded. "I have to trust them, right?"

"I could move you to a safe house."

"We agreed this is for the best."

"And yet, you're still being chased and attacked and shot at."

She poked a finger against the solid wall of his chest. "And yet, you've managed to protect me in spite of that."

"I'm serious, Rikki."

"So am I," she said. "And starting tomorrow, I'm calling all of my clients and setting up the appointments I had to cancel. I'm tired of hiding."

"You can't go back to work yet," he said, shaking his head.

"I can and I will." She stared him down. "Maybe if I go on with my life, someone will slip up and we can catch them."

"Or they'll kill you."

"They want something and they think I might have it. I get that and I sure know the danger. But I can't become a prisoner here, Blain. I'd gladly give them what they want if they'd leave my family alone."

"Or they could just want *you* dead." He touched a hand to her cheek. "Rest and we'll talk about our options tomorrow."

She thought about their kiss. "Like we have any options."

"There are always options." He gave her a smile and then turned to get back in his truck.

Rikki stood there, flanked by two guards, and watched him leave. And she had to wonder, what options *were* left for her and Blain?

FOURTEEN

Blain pulled his truck onto the driveway of his parents' house and stared up and down the quiet street. It was early morning. The homes along this street were small and age-worn but the people were hardworking and good. They watched out for each other.

Now he prayed his dad would help him. He needed honesty and clarity. He needed a break in this case. Being so embedded in all the Alvanetti drama and intrigue was beginning to weigh on him.

Being near Rikki and knowing they didn't have a future together was tearing him apart, mainly because he'd never in his wildest dreams wanted a future with the daughter of an alleged criminal. He hadn't slept much last night. Instead, he'd gone over the details of this case and he still didn't have any answers. Rikki was in danger but now, he had to wonder if the killer would take out her family members, one by one, until he or she had what they needed.

The front door of the brick Florida cracker house opened and his mom came out with a cup of coffee, her smile as serene as always. She wore her old chenille robe and flannel pajamas.

He'd have to remember to buy her a new robe for Christmas.

Getting out of the truck, he smiled. "Is that for me?"

His mom brought him the big blue mug. "Of course. Saw you sitting out here and since I had to get the paper, anyway…"

Blain reached down and retrieved the paper, memories of his own early morning paper route as a teen coming to the surface, and then took the mug full of steaming coffee. "Thanks, Mom. Is Dad up yet?"

"So that's why you're here."

"Yeah. I need to talk to him."

"He's watching the morning news." She tugged her robe close. "Let's get inside and I'll make us some breakfast."

Blain took a long sip of the coffee and followed his mom past the wooden white nativity scene by the boxwood shrubs. He didn't have much of an appetite but he'd eat his mother's cooking. Because this morning, he thanked God for being blessed with good parents.

Even if his dad had the one big flaw regarding the Alvanetti clan. But now Blain could drop some of his self-righteous judgments. Because lately, Blain seem to have acquired that same flaw.

He found Sam at the kitchen table, his gaze glued on the twenty-four-hour news channel's latest updates. "Hi, Dad," Blain said before sitting down across from him.

Sam's eyes narrowed. "Morning. You're out bright and early."

"Yeah, got to see the frost on the grass and everything."

While Mom cooked eggs and bacon and browned toast, Blain and his dad caught up on the news and sports, neither of which they agreed on.

Then they ate their breakfast and made more small talk. Finally Mom got up and cleared the table. "I'm going to get dressed. I've got an altar committee meeting at church."

She gave Blain a pat on the arm and then left with her second cup of coffee.

Sam drained his cup and then put his hands together on the poinsettia-themed plastic tablecloth. "What's up, son?"

"I need to tell you something in confidence," Blain said, hoping he'd made the right decision. "And then I need to ask for your help."

His dad cleared his throat and turned the television to mute. "I'm listening."

Blain told him about what had happened on the bay road. "I saw the driver, Dad. It was Billy Rogers."

Sam's silvery eyebrows shot up. "Billy Rogers? That hotshot rookie sheriff's deputy?"

"Yessir. It was dark but he was driving the car. He opened the door to check and see if they were bogged down. I saw him clear as day in the car's interior lights."

"Are you sure?" Sam asked. "It was rainy and dark. You said so yourself."

Blain had expected some disputes on this. "I saw him. I've known him since we were kids. It was Billy."

Sam stared out the window. Blain's mom, Catherine, had put a bird feeder out by the small patio. Two redbirds were perched on the bright stone, pecking away at their breakfast. A small yard flag swaying on an iron garden post showed a smiling Santa in a hammock and proclaimed "Christmas in Paradise."

Cute, but all Blain could think about was murder in paradise.

After a couple of moments, Sam glanced over at Blain. "If you say it's him, I'll go with that."

Blain didn't respond at first. He hadn't realized he was holding his breath until his dad continued. "So if the person you saw was Billy Rogers that means we've got a corrupt deputy in the department."

Blain bent his head, relief washing over him. "Yessir."

"What do you want me to do?" his dad asked, his dark eyes mirroring Blain's. "Just between you and me, I mean?"

"Watch," Blain said. "Listen. Observe. Ask around. You still have some pull and you can come and go without anyone wondering why you're hanging around."

"Good old-fashioned police work," Sam said. "I think I can handle that."

Blain stood up. "Do you think I'm doing the right thing here, Dad? You know how I feel about the Alvanetti family."

Sam stood, too. "You're doing your job. You're the lead detective and Regina Alvanetti seems to trust you."

"I'm the only available detective," Blain pointed out. "She has to trust me."

Sam chuckled as they walked toward the front door. "When it comes to the Alvanetti family, trust does not come easily."

One day when this was all over, Blain would ask his dad about that. He needed to hear more about what had happened with his dad and the Alvanettis. Because the more he learned about them, the more he realized he might have misjudged his father.

And maybe the Alvanettis, too. But he still needed more proof to give in to that assumption.

They made it to his truck and he showed his dad the dents and scratches the vehicle had received last night. "I've got someone running the partial on the license plates. I should have that when I get to the station."

"I'd like to know that myself," Sam said, his eyes scanning the neighborhood with a cop's habitual awareness.

Blain opened the truck door. "What do you know about Santo Alvanetti, Dad?"

Sam shook his head. "Not much. He took over the business at about the time I retired. He lives not far from his parents in a big modern house. On the bay side, I think."

Blain processed that tidbit. "I might ride out there and have a look around. He told us yesterday that his wife left him."

"You don't say? I heard he married a woman from Miami. Rumor has it she came from a very influential family."

"Just one more rabbit hole to go down," Blain said. "Somebody is after something but I can't figure out what it might be."

Sam braced one foot on the truck's bumper. "There is a lot of 'somethings' in that family.

Big house, barns, the warehouse. Lots of places to hide things and keep secrets."

Surprised yet again at this change in his dad, Blain asked, "What are you saying, Dad?"

"I'm saying somebody might be after something that is valuable. Highly valuable."

"Okay, we've established that but why come after Rikki?"

"Think about it, son. She travels in circles where everything is valuable and expensive. Her clients are wealthy and some of them have questionable work ethics. She's in their homes and she orders all kinds of furniture and, you know, those artsy pieces rich people like. No telling what she might see moving through. Or what she might be hiding."

"So is that what this is about?" Blain asked. "Shift the suspicion back to Regina and take it off the rest of the clan?"

His dad shook his head. "That is not what I meant at all. If Regina, or Rikki as you like to call her, found an important artifact that could have been stolen or possibly misplaced, she might try to hide it until she could do right by reporting it."

"And yet she hasn't done that—at least not with me."

Now he was doubting Rikki again.

"I'm looking at all the angles. You know to do that," Sam said.

Blain remembered Rikki saying she was going to call some of her local clients and get back to work. "We went through a long list of people she planned to meet with. She still wants to do that but I've cautioned her against it." He shrugged. "Maybe I should let her follow through as long as I'm around to protect her."

"It might get the ball rolling," Sam said. "Especially if there is something hidden in a shipment to her or to one of the houses she's decorating."

Blain nodded. "I'll dig a little deeper in that area."

"Maybe you can tie a couple of things together."

"I hope so. We've at least ruled out the victim's boyfriend and brother." Blain left, his mind whirling with so many scenarios he felt a headache coming on.

When he passed the Millbrook Lake Church, he saw Preacher's car parked there. Maybe he needed to consult with one other person on all of this. Just for good measure.

Rikki sat by her mother's bed, her mind full of turmoil. Santo had promised to check on their father at the hospital. She hoped he'd do that soon since news of Franco Alvanetti being attacked at the warehouse had been all over the local airwaves.

Now the whole state would know what was going on.

She didn't have to be a cop to know that would put her family in even more danger.

When Sonia moaned and opened her eyes, Rikki leaned close and took her mother's hand. "Hi, Mama. How are you this morning?"

"Tired," Sonia replied. "Did Victor come home last night?"

Victor? Rikki rubbed her mother's cold hand. "Victor is in Europe, remember? He's not here, Mama."

"He knows. He knows," Sonia said, agitation in each word. "Can't help it. Can't."

"Mama, it's okay," Rikki said. "Victor's not here and everything is okay. Are you in pain?"

Sonia opened her eyes and looked up at Rikki. "For you, darlin'. I did it for you. Always."

Daphne came in with Sonia's breakfast and a medicine tray. "Good morning," she said to Rikki.

Rikki nodded at the nurse. "She's not making sense," she said under her breath. "She's worried about Victor."

Daphne's brown eyed gaze moved from Rikki to Sonia. "The medication can make her disoriented. If we could get her outside in the sunshine, she might rally around more."

Rikki glanced out the big doors of the bedroom. "I wonder if I sat with her on the private patio. Do you think it's too chilly out today?"

Daphne stared out at the sun-dappled courtyard. "Not out there. The temperature is supposed to be in the high sixties today and with that sunshine, I'd think you'd be okay. We can bundle her."

Rikki checked her mother again. "Mama, Daphne's brought your breakfast. Time to sit up and take a few bites."

Sonia lifted her head and smiled at Daphne. "You've changed your hair."

Daphne gave Rikki a strained smile. "I got it cut."

Rikki couldn't remember anything about Daphne's hair changing recently. Maybe she'd worn it longer before Rikki arrived here. "It's cute," she said for her mother's benefit.

"I like it," Sonia replied. "Do I smell bacon?"

Rikki and Daphne both smiled. "Yes, you do," Rikki said.

Soon they had Sonia sitting up in bed, laughing and talking. When Rikki suggested they sit out in the small, enclosed courtyard by the bedroom, Sonia clapped her hands in glee. "I love my garden. Tomorrow we'll weed the rose garden and prune the camellia bushes."

"Yes, tomorrow," Rikki said.

She and Daphne helped Sonia into her wheelchair and bundled her in a robe and shawls and a heavy blanket. Then Rikki put a hat over Sonia's white-blond hair.

The sun did feel good out in the courtyard. Normally this space was surrounded by elephant ear and banana tree plants but they'd died back so the gardener had trimmed them for the winter. But a few hearty palm trees and camellia bushes gave the space a cozy feel.

After a few minutes of small talk, Sonia turned to Rikki and smiled. "You know, that family Bible is important to me. Don't lose it."

"Which Bible, Mama?" Rikki asked. She really needed to go over her mother's medication list and consult with Sonia's doctors. Maybe Daphne was right. Maybe the medicine was contributing to her mother's incoherent mumblings.

"That big one," Sonia said. Then she looked past Rikki, back toward the open bedroom doors. "Well, hello, good-looking."

Rikki whirled to find Blain standing there, staring at them with a definite frown of disapproval.

"Hello, Mrs. Alvanetti," he said, his eyes on Rikki. "Nice day to sit in the garden, isn't it?"

Sonia nodded and smiled. "Yes, it is. Do I know you?"

"I'm Blain Kent," he said as he walked out onto the brick-covered patio. "I work for the Millbrook Police Department."

"You know Alec, don't you?"

Surprise swept over Blain's face. "Yes, ma'am, I do."

"And that adorable Preacher Rory, right?"

"He's one of my best friends. In fact, I just left seeing him."

"He prays for me," Sonia said on a chuckle. "We all need that."

"Yes, we do," Blain said. "How do you know I'm friends with Alec and Preacher, Mrs. Alvanetti?"

"Alec bragged about you when he attended your cousin Beatrice's wedding here last spring."

Rikki gave Blain a shocked stare. "You remember that, Mama?"

Sonia pulled a face. "Of course I do. I gave Alec a big check for his foundation. The Caldwell Canines Service Dog Association."

"That's right," Blain said, shrugging toward Rikki. "I'm sure he appreciated it."

"You were here that day, Rikki," Sonia said. "Remember the key, darlin'?"

Rikki shook her head. "No, Mama. I left early. I'm not sure what you're talking about."

Daphne came through the doors and brushed past Blain. "Time to rest for a while. You might get sunburn if we don't get you back inside."

Sonia shook her head. "I like it out here."

Rikki stood. "Daphne's right, Mama. We've been out here for almost an hour."

Blain helped to get Sonia back into the bedroom but Daphne waved Rikki and him away. "I've got this. I'll get her a bath and get her all tucked in. You two go ahead and visit."

Rikki took Blain back toward the den. "That was interesting. She hasn't stayed up that long in a while. And she was making some sense today."

She wanted to tell Blain everything her mother had said to her but he seemed intent on something else. "What is it?"

He pulled her down on the couch and held her hands. Then he pulled her so close, she could smell the fresh air on his skin. With a whisper in her ear and a finger to her lips for her to stay quiet, he said, "The car that tried to run us off the road the other night? Even though he wasn't driving it, it was a rental registered to your brother Victor Alvanetti."

FIFTEEN

Shock caused her to stiffen and pull away. "But he's not here."

"Or so we thought," Blain said, still whispering. "I've ID'd the man who was driving the car but we don't know who the passenger was. I know I saw two people in the car, though."

"I did, too," she said, getting up to pace in front of him. Then she hurried back and sat down close to him so she could keep her words low. "Do you think the other one could have been Victor?"

"I don't know yet. We can't locate the vehicle but we've put out a search. I have a feeling the car is long gone but we're bringing in the driver and I'm going to interrogate him later today."

"Who is he?"

"I can't say right now," he said, motioning with a finger as he pointed up and around. He mouthed, "Bugs."

Bugs? Now he thought this house was bugged, too? No wonder he'd insisted on whispers.

"Can you get away for a while?" he asked, louder now.

"I think so. Daphne's here. I wanted to go and check on my father since I haven't heard from Santo this morning." She checked her watch. "It's midmorning. He should have called by now."

"We can do that." He stood and lifted her up and into his arms. "Go and check with the nurse and then meet me back here."

Rikki hurried to her mother's room but Sonia was already asleep. After she explained that Detective Kent was escorting her to see her father, Daphne tucked in her mother and came to stand with her near the door.

"I gave her the usual sedative for pain. She should sleep until dinnertime."

Rikki gave her mother a kiss and thanked Daphne. "I'll be back in a couple of hours."

"Take your time," Daphne said, her tone a tad impatient.

Deciding Daphne didn't like people hovering while she did her job, Rikki went to her room and grabbed her purse and a light jacket.

Blain was checking his phone but glanced up when she returned. Together, they walked outside. Rikki alerted the guards that she was leaving and sent one of them to sit inside in case Daphne and her mother needed anything.

"What's really going on?" she asked Blain when they were in his truck. "You're not in your official vehicle."

"I went by my folk's house for breakfast and came straight here," he told her. "I got the call about the car's registration right after I left there."

Then he took her hand. "And I just needed to see you and make sure you're all right."

"I am today," she said, the warmth of his touch giving her strength. "I tried not to think about last night and everything else that's happened to me lately." She stared out the window as the truck moved up the shell-encrusted land toward the iron gate. "I keep remembering Chad and how he tried to control me. What was he up to? Why was he here? He's dead now and I should feel something, but I'm so numb and in shock I honestly don't know what to feel."

"You and he were close for a while, so it's natural to mourn him. Someone murdered him and that's cause for you to be concerned for your own safety."

"Any idea who might have done this?"

"No answers on that one yet. It might take a while for the medical examiner to give us a cause of death or any other clues."

"Two people I knew just wiped away. It's not fair, Blain."

"No, it's not, but evil doesn't care about that." He gave her a solemn stare. "We have to hold out hope that God will see us through. That together, we can figure this out."

Her cell rang and Rikki jolted up in the seat. "It might be Daphne," she said. But when she saw the caller ID, her pulse shot up. "It's Santo."

"Can you come to my house?"

"Santo?" She glanced at Blain and saw the question on his face. "What's wrong?"

Her brother heaved a sigh. "I'm here with the kids and Lucia is sick with a horrible cold. I need to work and check on Papa, but my sitter didn't show up."

"And you want me to come?"

"Yes. I know you're not supposed to leave but maybe you can get someone to come with you?"

Rikki could hear children in the background. Little Nate was just a toddler and Lucia and Adriana were eight and six. How could Althea leave her children?

After explaining to Blain, she gave him a beseeching stare. "Lucia was a toddler when I left and now she's eight. Adriana and Nate don't even know me. I have to go, Blain."

"Then I'll be the one to take you."

He turned the truck to the left instead of heading back toward the hospital. "And you can call and check on your father while we're driving."

"Okay." She told her brother they were on the way. After she ended the call, she shook her head. "I don't see how a mother could leave her little children like that. What is wrong with my family?"

"Good question," Blain said. "Hopefully, we'll soon get the answer to that question and all the others we have."

Blain took in the striking modern house sitting on a low bluff over the bay. The stark white tri-leveled home was a contrast from the Alvanetti mansion up the road. This one was more glass than wood, with calculated symmetry and shifting roof lines. He could see the sparkling blue water straight through from the massive glass doors and the wall of windows across the back of the house.

"Impressive," he said to Rikki.

"Althea's dream house." She glanced around at the oleanders and sago palms. "And now she's nowhere to be found."

Blain made a note of that. "Interesting."

"You don't think—"

He didn't answer the question since the door swung open and Santo Alvanetti stood there looking rumpled and frazzled in jeans and a white button-up shirt. He gave Blain a hostile glare and then focused on Rikki. "Thanks for coming."

Rikki and Blain entered the big open foyer, the sounds of children coughing and calling out echoing up into the rafters of the house. Blain took in the polished wooden stairs and the high ceiling where a glass-and-wood light fixture bigger than his truck hung suspended in an artsy display. An open gallery ran around the second floor, allowing for a stunning view of the entire house. A massive Christmas tree stood on one side of the staircase, surrounded by presents all wrapped with matching paper and bows. And toys of various sizes and shapes littered the entryway and moved like a trail of colorful crumbs toward the back of the house.

When he heard more screaming and crying, he followed Santo and Rikki to the left where a large family room furnished with a white leather couch and two bright blue wing chairs seemed to be command central. The couch had splashes of a bright red goop on it and the chairs were smeared with what looked like the remains of canned spaghetti noodles.

The kitchen across the way was even worse. Dirty dishes everywhere and the distinct odor of burned toast lingering in the air. The row of windows displayed an infinity pool and a panoramic view of the water below. A big, furry dog barked to be let into the house.

And then there were the kids. The oldest, Lucia, as Rikki had called her, lay on the couch wrapped in a blue-and-white throw. Her expression exhibited dismay and fear.

Blain could identify with those feelings. He'd never been good with kids. He'd never thought about having any children.

But then, he'd never thought about being a family man until he'd met Rikki.

Another little girl ran to Rikki and started crying.

Rikki lifted the child into her arms and patted her dark head. "Adriana, I'm your aunt Rikki." She looked over the child's head at Santo. "She was a baby when I left."

"You've missed a lot of things," her brother said with a growl.

Blain watched Rikki with the little girl and his heart seemed to grow two sizes. He pushed at the emotion roiling through his system like a giant wave. He needed to get his head back in this investigation.

"What can I do to help?" he asked Santo, hoping to take his mind off things he couldn't have.

The other man shook his head and looked around. "Do you know how to change diapers?"

"Not really," Blain said. "But I do know how

to clean a kitchen and I'm pretty good at removing food stains from furniture."

Santo's look of appreciation marked yet another twist in this case. Maybe Blain's dad was right. Maybe the best way to get to the truth was to keep plugging away and earn the trust of this family. Blain could be wrong about them, but someone was definitely after the Alvanetti family for a reason.

He'd help get this situation under control and then he'd sit down with Santo and Rikki and see if he could get them to talk to him. About anything and everything.

A couple of hours later, Rikki had bathed Adriana and Nate and made sure they had a good lunch. Then she'd put them both down to rest. Adriana was reading picture books in her room and Nate was drifting off in his race car bed. Now she was sitting with Lucia. She'd checked the little girl's temperature and made her a bowl of chicken soup. Then she'd called the pediatrician and gotten advice on which over-the-counter cough syrup to use.

Now she watched as Blain cleared the kitchen and made sandwiches for the grown-ups. He'd also cleaned the floors, stacked the toys in a corner and sprayed the whole pile with disinfectant and somehow managed to get the tomato-sauce stains out of Althea's prized French blue high-back chairs.

Amazing. He'd been a real trouper. She knew he was a good man but seeing him in such a domestic situation made her dream of her own home and a man like Blain helping her with their children.

"I called the hospital," Santo said after coming downstairs. He'd had a shower and now wore a clean shirt and jeans. "Papa is awake and demanding to be released."

"That's good to hear," she said, blinking away the scene she'd just envisioned. "Can you go and pick him up, Santo?"

Her brother glanced around. "Yes, as long as you can hold down the fort here."

"We can do that," Blain said from the kitchen. "But before you leave, could I have a word with both of you?"

Santo put his hands on his hips and stared at Blain. "Is this important?"

"Yes," Blain said. "It involves my investigation."

Rikki shot her brother a warning glance. "Let me get Lucia settled in her room." She kissed the girl's head. "Is that okay, honey? Ready to take a nap now?"

The little girl bobbed her head. "Will you come up and check on me, Aunt Rikki?"

"Of course, sweetie." Rikki got up to help Lucia but Blain was there.

"Let me." He smiled at Lucia. "Wanna go for a ride up the stairs?"

Lucia's shy smile gave him his answer. He lifted her into his arms. "You can be like a little bird."

Rikki checked her brother but Santo's scowl had turned to mush as he watched his daughter laugh. His eyes went misty and he turned away.

"I'll be right back," she said, touching Santo's arm.

Then she followed Blain up the stairs and heard him ask where the princess lived. Lucia told him which room. By the time she and Blain had Lucia tucked in, Rikki's heart had told her what she'd been trying to deny. She might be falling for Blain Kent.

When they got back downstairs, Santo was sitting in a dining chair staring out at the water.

Rikki sat down beside him. "Why did Althea leave?"

He pushed at his thick black hair, his eyes filled with a faraway look. "She hasn't been happy lately. We fight a lot. She said she was just going to visit her family but I know she's not coming back."

"What about her children?"

"She's not concerned about them right now."

Blain sat down across from them and Santo clammed up and went back to staring out the window.

"So," Blain began, his notepad out on the table, "which one of you wants to go first? Somebody needs to level with me. I need the truth, and I mean all of it. I think maybe you both know who might be coming after you but you're afraid to tell me."

Surprised, Rikki shook her head. "You know that's not correct, Blain. If I knew who was doing this, I'd tell you in a heartbeat."

Blain's inky gaze moved over her. "I'd hope so." Then he nailed Santo with a hard glare. "What about you?"

Santo rubbed his eyes and looked down at the table. "I have my suspicions," he finally said. "I think our brother Victor *might* be involved."

Rikki's breath left her body. "Victor?" She turned to Blain. "Maybe he did rent that car that tried to run us off the road."

Santo's gaze moved from Blain to her. "Like I said, *mia sorella*, you've missed a lot of things."

SIXTEEN

Blain sat straight up. "We've been trying to locate your brother and you did tell me you might be able to find him. We have reason to believe he's back in this area."

Santo nodded. "I tried to talk to him but he's not taking my calls and my sources say he's evading them at every turn. I'm concerned about him and I'm worried about my wife being away during all of this. I have to protect my children."

"Do you think your children are in danger?" Blain asked.

"I pray not," Santo said. "These last few weeks have been crazy."

Rikki got up and started pacing. Then she whirled on her brother, her hands gripping the wooden chair in front of her. "What do you know, Santo?"

Santo sank back against his chair, weariness and resolve showing on his face. "The only thing I know for sure is that our company is in trouble. Between my issues with Althea and Mama's sickness, I've been preoccupied over the last few months. And of course, I have Papa on my back on a daily basis, too."

Rikki's guilt showed on her face. "And I haven't been here to help. You should have called me."

Santo expression hardened. "Why? So you could tell me how horribly we treated you and that you wish you'd never been born into this family?"

A hurt darkened her eyes. "Okay, I get that I've been deliberately distancing myself from all of this, but I'm here now. I want to find out who's trying to kill everyone I love and I want the truth. All of the truth."

Blain took notes and studied Santo. He did look haggard and tired. He also looked broken. "What kind of trouble is the company in?"

"We're losing money," Santo said. "Detective, I believe you want to find something to pin on us but once I took over the company, I tried to clean things up. I run a legitimate company now but it's not easy. My wife is angry at me because the money isn't rolling in. I can't make her understand I want something better for my children. I want honesty and integrity and dignity. Kind of hard to put a price on those things."

Rikki stared down at her brother as if she

didn't even know him. "Are we going to lose the business?"

"Not if I can help it," Santo replied. "I like what I do and I'm good at it. I just need some time to bring things around."

"So…does that mean you'd do anything to save Alvanetti Imports?" Blain asked.

"No, I won't stoop to anything illegal. That was the old days before my father had a change of heart. This is now. I'm concerned someone else is possibly after the company and maybe they're going about trying to fix things in their own way. And that someone could be Victor. He's lived off the family funds for a long time now but he's also had his own thing going on the side."

Blain scratched his head. "What kind of thing?"

"I'm afraid Victor might be into smuggling," Santo said. "And our business is the perfect cover."

"So when you mentioned possible smuggling to me last night, is this what you meant?"

"It's just a thought," Santo said. "A natural conclusion."

Rikki leaned down over her chair. "So you're saying that Victor is possibly doing illegal things and that he might be the one behind Tessa's death? And Chad's?"

"I don't know," her brother said, slapping his hand against the table. "I can't prove anything and…he's our brother. I don't want to accuse him if he's not the one."

Blain saw Rikki's pale face. "Hey, sit down. We'll find a way out of this."

"Can we?" she asked as she fell onto her chair. "What if this is Victor?"

Santo's dark eyes widened. "Our brother has done many things but he wouldn't murder an innocent woman. But he knows a lot of shady people and that bothers me."

Blain decided he should have been concentrating on the smuggling angle even more. "And what about Tessa?"

"What do you mean?" Rikki asked.

"Could she have known anybody who'd want something from you? A painting, some kind of artifact or expensive bauble?"

"I don't think so." Rikki shook her head. "Tessa was a good person."

"But can you ever really know all there is to know about a person?" he asked.

Her eyes went dark again. He'd pierced through her worst fears. "I don't know. You tell me, Detective."

Santo missed the moment and plunged ahead. "Your boyfriend could have known Victor, too."

He turned to Blain. "You should check around Presley's restaurants in Miami and Tallahassee."

"He never mentioned knowing either of you," Rikki said, her tone full of anger. "And I never brought him home."

"I've got someone looking into several different possibilities." Blain saw the distress on Rikki's face and the mirrored concern on her brother's face. "Did you find anything missing after you inventoried the warehouse?"

"No," Santo said. "I wasn't able to supervise everything but last night after everyone cleared out my workers did a thorough job and found nothing missing."

"If something were missing or say, someone was searching for something, what would be most likely?" Blain asked.

Santo shrugged. "We bring in all sorts of items. Rugs, paintings, jewelry, purses, furniture. You name it."

"Jewelry. That's easy to hide." Blain was grasping at straws but he had to start somewhere.

"Or easy to hide something in if it's a locket or a jewelry box," Santo said. His phone buzzed. "It's the hospital. I'd better go and get Papa."

He got up and then turned back. "Rikki, thank you for coming to help me. I've taken a lot for granted lately. That won't happen again."

"So have I," she said. Then she walked over

and hugged Santo, taking him by surprise from what Blain could tell.

"Are you going to get Althea back?" she asked.

"I don't know," Santo responded. He checked his watch. "The babysitter should be here in about twenty minutes, if she's not late again."

Blain waited until Santo went out the front door and then he turned to Rikki. "What do you make of that?"

"I believe him," she said. "I've never seen Santo like this. Both of my brothers have always been confident to the point of being arrogant. But he looks broken, Blain. Completely broken. I never knew he truly cared about the company and that he wanted to make things right."

Blain tugged her close before he could stop himself. "Well, he seems determined and he did open up to me. This information gives us some teeth. We have a connection now between Tessa's murder and possibly your brother. We can get on this and try to find Victor. Unless both of your brothers are in cahoots."

"But I can't believe that they'd kill Tessa and Chad. This is why I had to get away but I think instead of running from trouble, I created it." She pulled back and looked into his eyes. "You might search for Victor as Victor Kenneth Alvanetti. That's his full name. We all have nicknames. Rikki, Kenny and Sandy, although Santo hated his so we quit calling him that. And we haven't called Victor Kenny for a long time either."

Blain's antenna went up. "Did you say Kenny?"

Rikki lifted her chin. "Yes, why?"

"The *K* we found by Tessa's body."

"The bloody *K*," Rikki said, a hand going to her mouth. "Do you think she was trying to write my brother's name? Kenny?"

"Another question to add to our list," Blain said. "The letter looked like a *K* but it had a slash across it. Hard to say for sure."

Rikki sat down on the couch. "Both of my brothers as possible criminals. But it all started when I returned."

Pushing at her hair, she said, "I keep telling myself to get through this for Tessa's sake. Her killer needs to be locked up. And for Chad. He was a hothead and a jerk but he was murdered, too. We need justice for both of them and the guard who was shot."

"I agree." Blain didn't know what else to say. He wanted to kiss her and take her with him to a place where they could just relax and continue to get to know each other. But he had work to do, work that meant saving her and putting someone in jail.

Dragging her back into his arms, he held her there and then he did lean down and give her a quick kiss. When they heard a car outside, Blain stepped away.

But he did so with a new promise. "When this is over, Rikki, you and I have some things to get settled between us."

Her eyes went black with longing. "I hope that's soon."

"Yeah, me, too."

They let the babysitter in and Rikki took her up to see the kids and went over what needed to be done. Then they got in the truck and headed back to the Alvanetti estate.

That moment when they would both be free and clear of this mystery couldn't come soon enough for Blain. He wanted to be with Rikki Alvanetti. And that realization floored him more than anything else.

"At least no one followed us from Santo's house," Rikki said after they were back at the estate. "He should be here with Papa soon."

Blain did his usual thing, checking windows and doors, calling in to the station with an update and giving her covert glances that told her he was all in.

Oh, how she wanted to believe that.

Things had been different today. No one chasing or shooting unless you counted little kids and a big dog chasing each other. Her brother had it all. A family he loved, a solid position in the company and in society, a house with a million-dollar view.

And yet, he'd looked so defeated and dejected this morning Rikki had to wonder what price he'd paid. She wanted those things, too, but she didn't have to have the big house or the view. She'd settle for a little cottage in the woods.

With a small tree and a fireplace and Blain to hold her while she slept. Knowing that might not happen hurt as much as the pain of failing her family.

"All clear," Blain said. "I have to go file my report and put out some feelers on this latest. I've got a private detective on this case, too. Hope to hear from him soon."

Rikki motioned for him to sit. "Do you ever sleep?"

"Only when my eyes shut."

"I should go check on Mama. I know you need to go but stay until I get back, okay?"

"I'll be right here."

She hurried toward her mother's room and found Daphne checking her mother's vitals. "How is she?"

"She's been restless," Daphne said, her tone sharp as usual. "She's been asking for you. I'm glad you're here. Maybe you can calm her down."

"Okay. I'll sit with her a while." Rikki pulled

up a chair. "Oh, Daphne, Detective Kent is waiting for me. Would you send him back?"

Daphne gave her a curt nod and left. Rikki would be glad when Peggy arrived tonight. She and Peggy got along great but she thought Daphne judged her and condemned her at every turn.

"Mama, I'm home," she said. "It's Rikki. How are you?"

"Need to find the Bible."

"You want your Bible?" Rikki glanced around the room. It was neat and tidy but cluttered with medicine bottles and other sick-bed necessities. So was the adjoining bathroom. "I don't see it anywhere. Did Daphne put it away?"

"Library."

"It's probably not in the library, Mama. I'll check the nightstand." Her mother always kept her Bible nearby.

She was digging through the deep drawer when Blain walked in. "She's asking for her Bible and I can't find it."

"Want me to help look?"

"Check the other one," she said, indicating the matching nightstand on the other side of the bed.

Blain opened that one and looked inside. Then he rummaged around. Rikki checked and rechecked but only found some other books and papers in the one next to her mother's pillow.

Finally, she gave up and came around the bed. "Anything?"

Blain pulled out a necklace. "Nothing but this."

Rikki stared at the gold chain, confused. "That's odd. The centerpiece is missing."

Blain held up the heavy necklace. "Must have been a big gemstone, right? Was it real?"

"I don't think so," she said. The empty oval inch-wide circle looked damaged around the rim. "It's probably an old costume piece that she tossed in there and forgot. The stone must have popped out or gotten lost."

Blain handed her the damaged necklace. "Maybe you can find it around here somewhere."

Sonia moaned then and opened her eyes. "My necklace. You found it." But when she saw the necklace, she gasped, her hands going to her throat. "Where is the diamond, Rikki?"

Rikki looked from her mother to Blain. "I don't think it was a real diamond, Mama. You wouldn't keep something expensive in that nightstand."

Sonia fell back on the bed. "I need my Bible."

Rikki shook her head and motioned Blain to the hall. "I'd better try to settle her down. We have Bibles all over the house. I'll find one for her and read from it. Maybe the scriptures will calm her."

"I hope so," he said. Then he took the necklace back from her. "Have you ever seen this before?"

She shook her head. "I might have and just don't remember it. My mother is famous for her jewelry. She has several expensive pieces and a lot of costume jewelry, too. But lately, she hasn't worn much of it other than her wedding ring."

"Probably nothing," he said. "But just in case, I think I'll take this to be analyzed by the state crime lab, if you don't mind."

A jolt of fear hit at her already shattered system. "No, of course not." She moved further out into the hall. "But, Blain, you don't think someone's been inside my mother's room, do you?"

"I don't know," he said, his inky eyes holding hers. "But at this point, anything is possible."

Then he gave her a kiss on the cheek. "I'll check back with you later."

Rikki watched him leave, her mind on the necklace. Why would someone take only part of a necklace? Did they think the fake stone was real?

But then, how had someone managed to get inside her mother's room in the first place?

SEVENTEEN

"Hey, man, I've found out some interesting things about those two brothers."

Blain sank back in his squeaky desk chair and waited for Hunter Lawson to spill it. Which might take a while. Hunter did things on Hunter time.

"I'm listening," Blain said, rubbing his grainy eyes. No sleep and barely any time to eat.

"So Victor Alvanetti got in trouble a lot growing up. Petty theft in Miami, gun violations and drug use. He hooked up with a real big-time gang down there and worked his way up to some kind of lieutenant. Got banished to Europe by his powerful daddy when he overstepped his bounds. And word has it that he's even on his brother Santo's bad side, for flirting with his wife."

"That explains a lot," Blain said. "But we can't seem to find anything to pin this on Victor."

"Give it time," Hunter said through a grunt.

"Bad business, Blain. Apparently, Interpol is interested in him, too."

"For what?"

"Stolen artwork and artifacts, smuggling and reselling stolen items. But his little operation is falling on hard times."

"You've found out what I've been trying to find for days now. How'd you do that?"

"I have connections, bro. People who owe me." He laughed. "But none of this came from anybody in Europe. I kind of had to go into the belly of the beast."

Blain shook his head. He did not want to owe Hunter in a bad way or ever get on the man's bad side. But he knew he could count on Lawson to do what was needed and to stay within the law. Hunter had the same code of conduct as Alec and Preacher.

And you, he reminded himself. He couldn't step over that line, even to help a woman he was highly involved with. He'd find a way to save Rikki without losing his honor.

"Thanks," he said. After telling Hunter what Santo had told him, he urged Hunter to go on. "Okay, then, Victor is now number one on my suspect list. Whereabouts?"

"Now that's where things get interesting," Hunter said. "I've tracked him back to the good ol' USA."

Blain sat up. "Like Florida."

"That'd be my first guess."

"But how'd he get back without us knowing it?"

"That I can't answer yet. Later."

That ended the call.

Blain had never heard Hunter speak so much in one conversation. Hunter Lawson did not converse. But he did get down to business and fast.

But that revelation aside, he now had two immediate problems. One, the black sheep brother could be in the area and two, Rikki was even more vulnerable than ever. Had Victor been the one who'd possibility been rummaging around in her mother's room?

He'd question the very silent John Darty again and hopefully shake him up with this latest bit of news. If he could get Darty to spill the beans, he might be able to pin down one of them at least. And find out why they'd murdered three people to get at whatever they wanted.

"I have news, Darty," he said a few minutes later after a guard had let him in the suspect's jail cell. "I know who's been pulling your strings."

"I don't know what you mean," the greasy inmate said with a sneer. "You need to let me go, man."

"We caught you with a weapon that you'd just used to kill a man. Remember? Murder, attempted murder, use of an illegal firearm. Those charges along with your other crimes will have you sitting in a cell for a long, long time. But we will send you to a bigger, better place where you can make new friends."

Darty got a sick look on his face. "I want my lawyer."

"You'll get your day in court," Blain said. "Right now, you might want to consider helping yourself since the people who hired you are going to join you soon enough."

"I don't know what you mean," Darty said, his dirty fingernails doing a nervous dance on the old battered table top.

"I think you do," Blain retorted. "I'm working toward bringing in your boss. If you help me out, I might be able to cut you a deal."

"No dice," Darty said. "I can't help you."

"That's your choice," Blain told the man. "You'll go down with your overseer, then." He studied the man sitting across from him. "Or they'll let you take the fall if they don't have you murdered in your cell." He leaned in, his hands on the table. "That's how these people operate. If you don't do the job, they do you in."

Darty looked scared but refused to talk. "Either way, I'm going to prison," he finally said. "Not much I can do about that."

Darty's expression held a fatalistic expression

that almost made Blain feel sorry for him. He'd probably hoped to make a lot of money and skip town. Now he was facing a bleak future. What did he have to lose at this point?

"Look, Darty, we need your help. If you know anything that can lead us to Victor Alvanetti, tell me now. Do it as one last gesture of goodness."

Darty glanced around as if he were afraid someone was listening. "They wanted the woman out of the way. That's all I know."

Blain waited a beat.

"I might have heard something about a piece of jewelry. Worth a lot of money. A lot, man."

Blain got up and nodded. "You just shaved maybe five years off your sentence."

Darty didn't look too happy.

Blain told the chief what he'd heard and was about to call the lab about the necklace he'd found. When his phone rang, he saw Rikki's ID and answered immediately. "Hi. Everything okay?"

"Yes. My mother is more alert today. The doctor came to visit and he thinks she's improving. So that's good news. She keeps asking for her Bible, even though I found one and read to her."

"Glad she's better," Blain said. "Listen—"

"So, remember how I said I needed to get back to work?"

"Yes, but—"

"I've called a few clients and explained but most of them are aware of what's going on. Anyway, I did a few consults over the phone and internet but a couple of them want to meet in person."

"Rikki—"

"You can go with me, Blain." She finally stopped and took a breath while Blain wondered why everyone was so chatty today. "I need to work. I love what I do and now that my mother's better and Papa's on the mend, I thought I could try to find some sort of normal. I'm getting restless."

"It's dangerous," he said. "Too dangerous."

"Have you found anything? Did the necklace show any fingerprints?"

"No word on that yet. But…my private detective traced your brother Victor." He paused and took a breath. "I don't want to tell you this over the phone. How about lunch?"

"Lunch? Out in the open?"

"Yes," he said. "We'll be careful."

"I know you'll take care of me," she said. Then she added, "And Blain, I'll watch out for you, too. I'll see you in a bit."

Blain put away his phone and ran a hand down his face. He hoped he could take care of her and while he was touched that she wanted to do the same for him, he couldn't risk that. He prayed he'd be able to end this and soon. Chief Ferrier came bumbling over, his expression full of questions. "What you got now, Kent?"

Blain filled him in and let out a sigh. "I've narrowed it down to Rikki Alvanetti's brother Victor and I believe he's in the vicinity but I haven't told her that yet. Now she wants to get back to work, meet with clients. I don't like it."

The chief grunted. "No prints on that fake necklace, by the way. It came back clean. But her brother is after her, so we could set her up to flush him out."

"She'd do that. I think she wants to do that but I don't like that idea, either."

"Look, son, we need to end this," the chief said. "Nobody wants to deal with murder and criminals during the holidays. We got the Christmas parade tomorrow morning and I need every man on that."

Blain nodded. "My gut tells me they'll make a move of some kind when she leaves the house."

"And I can't spare you for protection detail much longer," the chief replied. "We can coordinate with the sheriff's department like we've been doing. Let me find someone else to work the Alvanetti detail for the weekend."

"I don't like that idea, sir."

He leaned on Blain's desk and pushed at his

bifocals. "I've heard things, Kent. Are you and the Alvanetti woman getting too close?"

Blain stood up. "You could say that, but don't worry. It's just a matter of time before all of this is over."

"All of it?" the chief asked.

Blain pulled a blank face. "Yessir. All of it."

He grabbed his jacket and headed out the door.

Thirty minutes later, he picked up Rikki and they drove to an out-of-the-way burger joint near the lake.

"My parents are taking it easy today," she said. "They both seem to be improving but Daphne promised to call me if anything changes."

"That's something," Blain said. "When had you planned on meeting with these clients you spoke with?"

"One later today and one tomorrow," she said. "If I'm allowed."

"I don't like this, Rikki. Your brother could be watching your every move. My PI tracked him back to the States and confirmed what we already suspected. Victor could be our man."

Her eyebrows shot up. "Are you sure?"

"Sure enough. Which is why you shouldn't meet with any clients right now."

"I'll be careful," she said. "I need to get back to work and I can't believe Victor is behind this."

"But someone is."

"You can go with me," she said after they'd ordered their food. Blain had a burger and she ordered a chicken salad.

"Can you change the appointment?"

"I'd rather not. It should only take long enough for me to measure and go over samples with my client."

The waitress brought their food and Rikki stared at her salad as if it was a bowl of bugs. "I can't believe this. If Victor wants something, why doesn't he just ask me for it?"

Blain chewed on a French fry. "I'm guessing it's the jewelry. Something that could bring a pile of money. Only, he doesn't want to ask nice. He wants to take it."

They ate in silence for a few minutes. Soft music played to soothe the lunch crowd, but Blain's nerves were all jumbled.

Finally, Rikki glanced up at him. "I don't think my brother will try to come after me if you're with me. It's a house out on the island. A newlywed couple. Meredith and Richard are nice people."

"How'd they get your name?"

"The client called me a while back since she knew I was coming to town. She told me they were interested in a complete overhaul."

Blain thought it over. "Today would be better

and I will go with you." He took a swig of his soda. "You have to understand, whoever this is, is probably watching your every move. They think you have that piece of jewelry."

"Well, then let's make them think I do. Draw them out and nab them."

"Don't play cop, okay. I'm still the point man."

She pushed her salad away after a few bites. "My own brother, possibly behind this. It doesn't make any sense."

"Do you know anything about your mother's expensive jewelry? I mean where she keeps it? Is it insured? Things such as that?"

"If she does have any valuable jewelry, it's all locked up. She's always told all of us we'd inherit her jewelry but I don't know which is which."

"I think someone thought they'd found the real deal and they took the stone from her bedside table. But now, they've realized that one was a fake and they need the real one."

"That's unbelievable. If Victor needed money, why didn't he just ask?"

"I think he did and everyone turned him down."

She pushed her food away and stared out the window.

Blain put his hand over hers on the table. "This was supposed to be a nice, quiet lunch. Sorry I told you all that."

"No, don't say that, Blain. Honesty is the one

thing I need right now. I've been lied to all my life, protected in the worst kind of way. But even a lie of protection is still a lie. I need to know the truth."

Blain saw the strength in her eyes. She wasn't like the rest of them. She wanted to do the right thing. She'd come home in spite of her family's sordid past, to be with her mother. And she'd even managed to get closer to her father and one of her brothers while she'd been here.

"You know, before I met you," he said, his fingers still touching hers, "I detested everyone in your family but your mother. She always stood as a symbol of good to me. But I never understood how she handled the alleged rumors that swirled around your family."

Rikki smiled and sipped her tea. "My mother has always been faithful and I don't think that will ever change. She fell in love with my father." She set down her tea glass. "I do believe she tried for years to change him. And while he's still not a churchgoer, I think he's mellowed. He let Santo take over and he seems determined to make things right."

"So you believe it's possible for a person to love another person even if that person is involved in something illegal or immoral?"

She pulled her hand away and gave him a perplexed stare. "Yes, I guess that's what I'm saying. Are you judging my mother because she fell in love with the wrong person? Or are you telling me in you're not-so-subtle way that you can't ever care about *me*, Blain?"

"No," he said, standing when she lifted out of her chair. "That's not what I'm saying."

"I love my family in spite of everything," she said, anger making her cheekbones turn pink. "I had to come to that conclusion the hard way. I lost my best friend and my ex-boyfriend."

"Yes," he said, slapping some bills on the table before he followed her to the truck. "Yes, you did. And now it looks like one of your brothers could be behind this. How will you react to him, Rikki, if that's the case?"

She whirled, one hand on the door handle of the truck. "I guess I'll visit him in jail and pray for him."

"Okay, all right." Blain reached up to touch her hair. "I'm sorry."

"No, I asked for honesty," she said. "And the truth is right here, glaring at me. No matter what happens with this investigation, one thing is for sure. You and I can never be together."

"Why not?" he asked, his heart aching in a way that he'd never felt before. "Why not, Rikki?"

She hopped up into the truck and turned to stare at him.

"Because I will always be an Alvanetti."

EIGHTEEN

Rikki waited to make sure Blain had left.

They hadn't talked on the drive back to the estate. She was still hurt that he'd ask a question that implied what he'd felt from the beginning. Her family was bad news, criminals and immoral people. That her sweet mother shouldn't have loved a man who ignored the rules and did whatever he wanted.

That Blain couldn't love a woman who had deep ties with what everyone considered to be a Mafia family.

But isn't that the reason you left?

Rikki went to her room and sat down in an armchair by the window that had a nice view of the pool and the vast lake beyond. Two seagulls flew across the water, their white wings glistening against the blue sky.

Yes, she'd left full of self-righteous indignation and a misguided determination to free herself from her father's massive shadow. But she'd also left because she was heartbroken and still grieving for her young husband who'd died too soon. He'd died and no one could explain to her why. And she'd left because she had to do things her way so she could make her *own* way in the world.

But had she done that?

She was successful and able to take care of herself but she'd paid a high price for breaking free. She'd made countless mistakes, Chad being one of those, and she'd missed years of being with her family, years she couldn't get back.

But you're here now. You can make a difference.

They all needed her. And maybe she needed to be needed. But did she need her family?

It was time she faced the fact that she *was* an Alvanetti.

So she slinked her way into her father's office and found the key to the gun cabinet. And then she picked out a pistol that she knew she could fire. Her brothers had taken her to target practice enough that she remembered the feel of a gun in her hands.

She'd protect herself. She'd always done that, emotionally. Now it was time to do it to end this horror she'd walked into.

If Victor showed up and tried to kill her, what would he gain? She didn't have any expensive jewelry. Just a few sentimental pieces that she loved and some artsy pieces that she'd bought from friends over the years. Nothing that would net a fortune. And she didn't remember her mother owning anything that would be that extremely valuable. Valuable enough to kill over, at least.

Tired of fighting, tired of running, she called her clients and asked to move their meeting up a couple of hours. Then she packed up the loaded gun along with her samples and her design ideas and started down the hallway to check on her mom.

"You can take a break, Daphne," she told the nurse. "I need to leave in a few minutes but we'll be fine until then."

Daphne gave her a rare smile. "Okay, I'll be back in fifteen minutes."

After sitting with Sonia for a while, Rikki leaned over to kiss her mother. "I love you, Mama."

Sonia opened her eyes and smiled up at Rikki. "I love you, too, darling. I always have. I love all of my children." She took Rikki's hand. "A mother's love is the strongest on earth." Sonia clung to her. "We have to do what we need to do to protect and love our children."

Rikki saw the fear in her mother's eyes. "Are you all right, Mama?"

Sonia slowly moved her head in a nod. "I'm

gonna pull out of this. I'll be back on my feet soon and everything will be better then. You'll see."

"I believe you," Rikki said. "I have some errands to run. I'll send Daphne back in and then I'll be back to check on you before dinner. If you're sure you'll be okay."

"I'm fine. Be careful out there," Sonia said, her eyes beginning to droop. Then she opened them again. "Did you ever find my Bible, honey?"

Rikki shook her head. "I'm not sure I know which one you want. I'll try again when I get back."

"And that key," Sonia said. "I need the key and the Bible."

"What key, Mama?"

"The key, darlin'." Sonia was drifting off. "The key I lost. Thought you had it."

"I only have my car keys and my house keys," Rikki replied.

"Check your purse," Sonia insisted. "Gold."

Her mother drifted off again.

More confused than ever, Rikki hurried into the kitchen area so she could grab a set of car keys. Maybe she'd find her mother's missing key there. Yet one more sign that her mother was still frail and disoriented. Rikki hoped it wasn't something worse.

"Where do you think you're going?" Franco called from his chair in the corner.

"I'm going back to work," she said, turning to walk toward him. His head was bandaged and he looked like he'd just woken up from a nap. "I'm tired of hiding."

Her father gave her one of his frowns. "Where is Detective Kent?"

"He has other things to do today."

Franco shook a finger at her. "You will not leave this property without a guard."

"Papa—"

"I mean it, Regina. Do you want to get yourself killed?"

Before she could respond, he pulled out his phone and issued an order. "Murphy will stay with you at all times."

When a giant of a man wearing a dark suit came through the door, Rikki wanted to scream her silent rage. Not that it would do her any good. Murphy didn't seem to blink at anything.

She hadn't planned for this. Rikki refused to wait for Blain to go with her, maybe because she wanted to prove to him that her own brother wouldn't kill her. But having one of her father's guards with her only made matters worse and proved Blain's point. The Alvanettis had their own code and they protected their own, no matter what it took.

Would her parents protect Victor? Was her mother trying to warn her of that possibility?

"You can leave as long as he's with you," Franco said, as if he were reading her thoughts. He pointed to Murphy. "Don't let her out of your sight."

Rikki stared at her father and then shot a frown toward the guard. "You have to stay outside while I'm conducting business."

Murphy grunted and gave her father a nod. "I'll stay in another room."

Rikki reluctantly gave in and followed the giant outside. Then she got in the back of a dark sedan and stared out the tinted window until they arrived at the beach house. They were late getting out here, due to the heavy weekend traffic but she saw another car in the narrow driveway.

At least she was doing something constructive. Something to take her mind off Blain and the memory of his dark, brooding expression when he'd left her earlier. He wouldn't like that she'd gone against his wishes, but what did it matter now?

She wasn't answering his calls.

Blain stared at his phone and wondered if Rikki would ever talk to him again. She'd seen through his efforts to get past her family dynamics but she hadn't allowed him to explain how his preconceived notions had changed over this last week.

She hadn't allowed him to explain anything. He might seem like the one with preconceived notions but she'd sure jumped to conclusions about him, too.

Now, his gut was burning with the sure knowledge that she'd go off in a tizzy and try to prove something to everyone. She was determined to either flaunt her courage to the world or to get herself into some hot water. That reckless streak *was* a true Alvanetti trait.

Blain asked God to keep her safe until he could get there, but then he figured God had this already. Still, his gut didn't want to accept that.

He was headed out of the police station when Chief Ferrier called to him. "Kent, get in here. We got some news."

Blain whirled to go into the chief's office. "What is it, sir?"

"The crime lab called. The blood on the statue is Franco Alvanetti's, but then, we figured that. But they managed to lift some partial prints, too."

Blain sat down. "And?"

"You won't believe this," the chief said. "Try Althea Alvanetti."

"What?" Blain rubbed a hand down his jaw, an alertness humming through him. "Are they sure?"

"Yes. Very sure. Apparently she had a checkered past before she married into the family. Her prints are on record for some shoplifting and other petty crimes back in the day."

"Amazing," Blain said. "So she tried to kill her father-in-law?"

"It looks that way," Chief Ferrier said. "Now we just gotta figure how to tie this to those other murders."

"Do you think she shot Chad Presley, too?"

"Don't know. We do know the slugs from both murders could have come from the same gun. Might be nice to find that gun."

Blain gave an affirmation on that. "Yep. We've got a partial on the shoe prints we found at both scenes and they seem to match, too. That could prove the same person was at Rikki's town house and out behind the warehouse."

"The murderer," the chief said, nodding.

"So the shooter could definitely be the same person."

"Yes."

Blain stood. "I have to get out to the Alvanetti estate. Regina Alavanetti is not happy with me right now. I think she might have bolted."

"As in, left the premises?"

"Yessir. She got mad at me earlier when I questioned her mother's loyalty to Franco."

"Maybe you punctured a hole in Miss Regina's loyalty, too."

"I think I did. And I believe she's just now realizing she is still loyal to her family." And so was he at the moment.

Chief Ferrier's bushy brows did their usual frowning slant. "You might want to keep digging, son. From what I hear, Sonia Alvanetti always wore the pants in that family. And I'm pretty sure she still does. I don't believe she's ever had a problem with what Franco does for a living."

Rikki and the hulking guard made their way up the wide steps to the broad porch of the stunning house out on Millbrook Island. Out here, the houses were big and spacious and pricey. The view of the Gulf of Mexico sparkled beyond the wide glass windows, the whitecaps crashing into bubbling foam against the creamy sand.

This house had been vacant for a while. What furniture the previous owners had left was sparse and covered with sheets. A blank slate for Rikki to decorate and pamper. She couldn't wait to throw herself back into work.

Murphy rang the doorbell and peered through the glass door at the empty entryway and the big room beyond. "I have to check things out," he said, indicating he would be going inside with her.

Rikki started to protest and then changed her mind. She was behaving like a spoiled brat, coming out here on her own. She didn't want to get Murphy shot, too. "Okay," she said, wishing now she hadn't been so impulsive and reckless. Wishing Blain was here with her in spite of their differences.

Blain cared about her. She knew that from his kisses.

She cared about him. She'd tried to show him that in her kisses and in all of her actions.

But it was too late to fret about Blain right now. When no one came to the door, she turned to Murphy. "They're supposed to meet us here. Maybe they're running late."

She turned to search for any other cars. A luxury sedan sat in the short drive but no other vehicles were on the property.

"Try again, Murphy," she said, her nerves wrapping around themselves.

Murphy rang the bell and then jiggled the door knob. The big door slipped open.

"Maybe they want us to go on inside," Rikki said.

Murphy blocked her from doing that. "Not yet, ma'am."

He went in ahead of her and walked like a shield in front of her through the sprawling one-level home.

"See? Nothing," Rikki said, relief washing over her after they'd checked every room. "I'm sure they're on their way. I can do some measuring and take notes while we wait." She gave Murphy what she hoped was a confident smile. "You could wait out on the terrace."

"I stay here," Murphy replied. "Where you go, I go."

"Okay, then you can hold the tape measure for me."

Soon Rikki was immersed in sketches and ideas. She typed notes on her electronic pad and got to know Big Murph—as he instructed her to call him. Murphy was soon laughing and talking and telling her about his six children.

"I never knew you had children," she said. She'd seen him through the years, always hulking around but she'd never actually talked to any of the guards much. While they went from room to room, she enjoyed their banter and promised herself she'd reach out to the people around her more.

"It's been thirty minutes," he said when they came back into the big kitchen and dining room area. "Whatta you want to do now?"

"I'll try to call again," she said, a dagger of

apprehension slashing through her. She left a message with the wife and then turned to Murphy. "I think this was a bad idea."

He pulled out his revolver. "Yeah, me, too. I got a funny feeling and it ain't a good one."

They were heading for the front door when it swung open and Althea Alvanetti walked in. "Hello," she said to Rikki. "Long time, no see."

"What are you doing here?" Rikki asked, a tremble of warning moving up her backbone. Her sister-in-law looked thin, her short white-blond hair curling around her cheeks. She wore a beige wool coat over winter-white pants. Her green eyes looked a little too bright.

"I thought Meredith would be here," Althea said on a serene smile. "I did recommend you to her, after all."

Meredith. The homeowner. A friend of Althea's. Rikki's stomach roiled in tune to the waves crashing below.

"She's late and we're leaving," Rikki said, reaching a hand in her bag to locate her loaded gun. "I thought you had left town. I heard you'd gone to Miami."

"Not yet," Althea said. "Not that you'd care."

Rikki gripped the weapon, not sure if she could shoot the mother of Santo's children. "I care about my brother and my nieces and nephew."

Althea's eyes flared hot. "Yeah, and you're

such a model of society. You left and never looked back until now."

"Althea, what do you want?"

"I told you, I came to see my friend."

Rikki wasn't buying that. Althea looked nervous. She kept glancing back over her shoulder. She paced back and forth, blocking the front door.

Murphy put a hand on his gun holster. "Miss Althea, don't make me have to pull out my weapon again."

"Shut up, Murphy," Althea said. "I'm not here to harm the little princess."

Rikki was about to push past her when a car pulled up. Hoping beyond hope that Blain had tracked her down, she glanced at the figure coming up the steps to the porch.

Her heart sank and she knew she'd made a fatal mistake coming here. Her brother Victor walked in, grabbed Althea in a hug and waved his gun toward Rikki and Big Murph.

"Take out your weapons," Althea said on a giggle. "Put them on the floor."

Sick to her stomach, Rikki stared at her brother. "I told them it couldn't be you. I defended you and everyone else in my family and I came out here today to prove them wrong."

"Joke's on you," Althea said. "He's with me

now." She laughed up at Victor then waved her gun. "Now put your weapons on the floor."

Rikki nodded at Big Murph. They both carefully laid their guns on the hardwood. Althea shoved the guns away with her booted foot and then smiled up at Victor. "I was right that she couldn't resist showing off her decorating skills."

Victor didn't respond. Instead, he gave Rikki a thoughtful stare. "You're a hard woman to pin down, Rikki," he said. "But…at last, I've found you."

NINETEEN

Blain couldn't get Rikki to answer. He tried the estate house phone. Daphne answered.

"Listen, Daphne, this is Detective Blain Kent. I need to speak to Regina Alvanetti. It's urgent."

"She's not here," the nurse said. "She left with one of the guards. She had an outside appointment."

Blain closed his eyes and let out a breath. "Do you know where they went?"

"No. One of her clients."

He heard someone talking in the background.

"I have to go," Daphne said. Then she hung up.

He could call one of the guards but there wasn't any time. So he pulled up the client list she'd given him. Five names. One was Alec Caldwell. He'd call him if he couldn't find her at the others. He called the next one on the list.

An older gentleman answered and went on and on about how wonderful she was and how much he loved his home. But he said he'd rescheduled everything with Rikki since she was dealing with family matters.

Blain hit the steering wheel, still sitting out in the parking lot. He couldn't call and drive at the same time, but he was sorely tempted. The next call went to voice mail. He decided not to leave a message. Too dangerous.

Three more.

A maid answered the next call and explained the owners were out of town.

Number four yielded a bubbly young mother who said she totally understood that Rikki couldn't work with her right now, so they'd decided to put things off until after the holidays.

That left the last one. He checked the address after that one rang and rang. Then he remembered what Rikki had told him. Althea had given her a referral. The island. The house was out on the island.

He cranked his truck and peeled out of the station parking lot. Then he radioed in and asked for backup.

Traffic out to the island was heavy. People rented condos during the weekend of the Christmas parade. And they'd already started coming in.

Blain hit the siren that he rarely used and tried to move past a long row of cars over the causeway bridge out to the barrier island on the Gulf of Mexico, sweat beading on his brow.

Dodging the sparse oncoming traffic off the island, he finally reached the old beach road and turned toward the mansions that lined the coast. But which one?

Searching on both the Gulf side on the left and the bay side to the right, Blain blinked and tried to focus. When he reached the curve that followed the shore, he saw a big stucco house with a massive set of wooden steps with ornate banisters. And two dark sedans parked in the wide gravel and shell drive. One of the sedans looked like one he'd seen at the Alvanetti estate.

This had to be the place.

Skidding onto the drive, he barely moved off the road before he jumped out of the truck and rushed up the stairs.

The front door stood ajar.

Blain's heart beat with a burst of adrenaline. He held his weapon up and pushed through the door, a silent prayer caught against each pounding of his pulse.

He checked the big open kitchen and living area and then carefully went through the empty rooms. In the last bedroom, he found a big man lying on the floor.

Big Murph. He worked for the Alvanettis.

"Murphy? You okay?"

Blain checked his pulse and found a solid beat. He had a nasty bump on his wide forehead and but other than that, Murphy seemed to be alive at least.

Blain called it in and then rolled Murphy over. "Hey, Murphy, can you hear me?"

The big man grunted and squinted up at Blain. "Detective?"

"It's me," Blain said. "Murph, what happened? Where is Rikki?"

Murphy moaned and blinked. "That Althea. She came in and then… Victor showed up. They took… Miss Alvanetti. Took my…gun and…hit me over the head." He winced. "I'm sorry. I tried but they took her away."

Blain held a hand on the big guard and stared out at the brilliant sunshine hitting the water. And he wondered what to do now. When he heard sirens coming up the beach road, he waited.

But he called Santo Alvanetti while he was waiting.

Rikki didn't know how to pray. She was so angry at herself and the world she wanted to scream out to anyone who'd listen. She wasn't mad at God because *she* was the one who'd decided to run again. To go out on her own and do what she thought was best, rather than waiting on the Lord and the protector he'd sent to guard her.

Stupid.

Her own brother and her sister-in-law, in this together.

How could her family ever recover from this?

The sun was setting toward the west as the big SUV flew up the two-lane road. Victor drove while Althea sat in the back with a gun to Rikki's head.

"Why?" Rikki finally asked, still dazed from being dragged down the long row of steps at the house. Her whole body throbbed in protest from being forced into this vehicle.

Althea's laughter was full of a bitter bite. "Why do you think? My husband has always been too noble for his own good. He never wanted any part of the family's business but he was forced to take over when your father became too senile and disinterested to keep things going. He changed everything and became what he calls legit. Now we're struggling day in and day out. It's not right."

"Santo is a good man," Rikki said, her gaze hitting Victor's in the rearview mirror. "He wants to do what's right."

"He's weak," Althea said, her vivid green eyes widening. "Just like his father."

"And what about you, Victor?" Rikki asked. "How could you ever stoop this low?"

Victor stared at her in the mirror, a flash of warning in his eyes. "I have my reasons."

Althea pushed the gun at Rikki. "And you sit in judgment of us. You have no idea what this family's been through since you left."

"As if I'm the reason for all of your choices," Rikki shouted. "I left because of things like this. The secrets and lies, the betrayal. You all killed Drake and now you'll finish me off. And why? Over some lost piece of jewelry?"

"Rikki, Drake drank too much and had a horrible accident," Victor said. "I wish you'd accept that."

"I can't," Rikki said. "And I can't accept this."

"She knows where the necklace is," Althea said to Victor. "That's the only reason I'm here."

Victor didn't say a word.

"I don't know anything about a necklace," Rikki said. "Why would I?"

"Your mother told Victor about it the day of the wedding and then she mentioned it again when she was in Europe," Althea said. "He thought she'd give it to him eventually since he's the oldest. But then she lost her marbles and had to be shipped home. I know she must have told you what happened to it after you suddenly decided to return to the fold." Althea dug the gun into Rikki's rib cage. "You have the key to that box."

"I don't have any necklace," Rikki said. But she now understood who'd been snooping in her mother's bedroom. "And I sure don't have a key."

"She's lying," Althea said, shouting up to Victor. "Sonia let it slip that she gave the key to Regina."

"We're heading to the town house now," Victor retorted. "So relax."

The key? Her mother had mentioned a key. Her Bible and the key. Were the two connected? She almost said something but decided to bide her time. If they were taking her to her town house, she might be able to escape somehow.

A few minutes later, Victor pulled the vehicle up to her house. "We have to hurry, Althea. Find the key and get out."

"I don't have a key," Rikki said again. They ignored her.

"You have a door key," Althea said. "Open it."

Rikki did as Althea asked, praying she could find a way out of this situation. Would they kill her if she didn't find what they wanted?

The house was eerily quiet, the Christmas tree looking lonely and forlorn and the smell of a sickly sweet cinnamon scent she'd once loved making her gag.

Althea forced her up to her room. "I want

you to find your gold purse," she said. "The one Sonia gave you last Christmas. You had it at the wedding."

Rikki's heart skidded. Her mother had mentioned the word *gold* to her earlier. She thought her mother meant a gold key. Now it was a gold purse?

"I can only think of one," she said as Althea shoved her into the closet while Victor stood watch. She tried to breathe, tried to put one foot in front of the other. But in her mind, Rikki was screaming for her brother to stop this and help her.

"Find it." Althea seemed to delight in holding that gun at her back.

Rikki searched until she found a square gold leather clutch that had to have cost a small fortune. The designer emblem flashed at her in a gaudy wink, making her wonder why she'd ever liked this purse in the first place. She'd left it here after the wedding, never dreaming her mother had placed a key inside.

"Look inside," Althea said, shoving at her again. "And hurry."

Rikki thought about hitting Althea over the head but Victor would just take over. Her silent prayers held her steady while she searched inside the deep pockets of the purse.

And felt a big key.

Althea pushed her against the closet door. "Give it to me now!"

Rikki pulled out the key. "Here. If it means so much to you, take it."

Althea grinned and shoved her out of the room. Rikki dropped the purse on the bed, hoping if Blain came here he'd find it out of place.

"Let's go, Victor," Althea said. "We need to get to the warehouse before dark."

Victor mumbled and gave Rikki a hard glare.

Her brother had turned into someone she didn't even know. Since when did he let Althea call the shots?

"You two deserve each other," she said as she went past Victor.

He didn't respond. Soon they were back in the SUV and zooming out toward the warehouse. The sun was beginning to set toward the west.

And with darkness, Rikki's chances of making it out alive would soon end. They had the key now. They'd kill her. They'd been trying to kill her all along, probably so they could get in her house and search it under the guise of being concerned family. She had no idea what they thought they'd find. She didn't have the necklace.

But her brother didn't seem concerned now.

He kept right on driving as if they were out for a leisurely ride.

Then her sister-in-law looked out the window. "Victor, we have to get to the warehouse before they find us."

"I need to talk to Mama," Victor said. "She might be able to tell us what we need to know about the jewelry case."

"Are you crazy?" Althea asked, disbelief sounding in her tone. "That old woman won't remember a thing."

"No, Althea," Victor said. "I know exactly what I'm doing. Mother has always been on our side. If we don't find the necklace tonight, I'm going to talk to her."

Confused, Rikki stared from her brother to her sister-in-law. "What do you mean?"

Althea laughed again, all of her anger gone now. "Your mother is one smart cookie. And she's probably not happy about the way things have been going lately."

"But she's too sick to even know what's going on," Rikki replied. "Just take the key and leave her out of this."

"She's forgetful," Althea replied. "But she's still the one in charge." Althea glanced up at Victor. "Do you think she's on to us?"

"Mother always knows what's going on," Victor said. "She knew which purse she put the key in, didn't she?"

Althea giggled. "I guess so. You did manage to get that much out of her. We have it now, anyway."

Rikki thought she might be ill. Could it be possible they'd all fooled her? Could her dear, sweet mother really be involved in this, too?

TWENTY

Blain paced back and forth inside the empty beach house. Murphy had been taken away in an ambulance but not before he'd given them a complete description of both Althea and Victor Alvanetti.

"It was them. They didn't even try to hide it."

Blain couldn't believe he'd missed the Althea angle. But how did Victor play into all of this? Was he in love with Althea?

"They talked about a necklace," Murphy said. "I heard 'em right before I passed out. Some necklace that could bring them millions of dollars."

Blain stopped in his tracks. That necklace had to be either at the Alvanetti warehouse or at the estate. At least all of the clues showed that someone had been searching for it at both places and at Rikki's townhome, too.

They'd sent a patrol over there right away. A report had come back that someone had been there. An empty gold purse was lying on the bed in Rikki's room.

He wondered if she'd gone by there or if whoever had her had left that purse there.

He turned and hurried to the chief. "I have to go."

"And where are you going?"

"To the warehouse and then the estate. I think the necklace could be at either location. And that means they might have her there, too."

"But she's been at the estate for several days now," the chief pointed out.

"But they didn't know where the necklace was hidden," Blain said. "I'm beginning to think they never wanted Rikki dead. They just wanted her out of the way so they could search for this mysterious necklace."

"So they killed people all around her to scare her?"

Blain nodded. "Or they killed people all around her because they panicked. Either way, if they have what they want now, they'll be done with Rikki."

Chief Ferrier frowned and pondered. "I don't know what you're doing, Kent, but you are sure up to your eyeballs in this case. You take someone with you wherever you're going."

"I will," Blain said, turning to leave.

"I'll go with him," a deep voice called out from a hallway.

Blain turned to find his dad standing there.

"Where did you come from?" he asked, surprised. He'd been waiting to hear back from his dad about Billy Rogers and now here he was.

Sam checked the hallway and then said, "I heard chatter on the radio. So I drove out and came in the door when you were in the back." His dad moved close. "I need to talk to you. Privately."

Blain wanted to leave but he walked with his father into a bedroom. Dad wouldn't halt him unless this was important.

Sam spoke into Blain's ear. "I have Billy Rogers handcuffed out in my car. And he's told me some very interesting things."

"Let's go," Blain said. He'd blinked and let Rikki walk right into a trap. He hoped Billy would give up the goods on the entire clan and right now, he didn't care whether they did things by the book or not.

Because the whole family was once again under suspicion.

Rikki yanked away from Althea's hold on her arm after they entered the back door to the warehouse. She'd tried to find a way to run but the night was so dark she feared she'd get lost in the thick woods near the river. That might be better than sticking around to die here, however.

She tried to get to the truth by talking. Maybe she could stall them. After they entered the warehouse, she said, "This is ridiculous. My mother has been ill for months now. She can't be in on this. She's been asking—"

She stopped and clammed up. She wouldn't give them any ammunition to use against her. The warehouse was dark and still, with large crates and boxes everywhere. She could hide here amidst the clutter until someone came for her. It was the only way.

"Asking what? What has your mother been telling you?" Althea said, whirling with the gun pressed to Rikki's chest. "You'd better tell me now."

"What are you doing?"

They all turned to find Santo staring at them from a dark corner near the hallway to the office. He flipped on a glowing yellow light that cast an eerie aura all around them.

"Santo?" Althea looked shocked. "What are you doing here?"

"I asked you first," her husband said, his tone flat, his eyes as black as coal. His gaze moved from Althea to Rikki and then back.

Althea faltered. "I…have business here. You should leave."

Santo stared at his wife. "And what business would that be since you left me and our children? Maybe I should ask Victor about that?"

Rikki tried to run to Santo, but Althea held her and pointed the gun to her head. Rikki spoke to Santo. "They claim Mama knows what's going on. They want a necklace that's worth a lot of money."

"Mama is safe at home," Santo replied, his tone as calm as the wind outside the window. "*I* have Daphne and a guard in her room. Our father is there with her."

"Daphne?" Althea's confidence was waning by the minute. "But she's—"

"In on this?" Santo asked, his dark eyes following his wife's every move. "I think you're wrong there, darling. I hired Daphne personally and she follows my orders. Not yours."

"What?"

Santo's calm, angry eyes met his wife's. "I'm not going to call in the law just yet. I'm giving both of you a chance to explain this first. So you'd better make it good."

Rikki saw the fear in Althea's cold eyes. Had she truly believed she'd get away with this? Rikki glanced from Althea to Victor. He hadn't spoken at all. But she saw a look passing between her brothers. A knowing look. What was going on around here?

"I'm waiting," Santo said. "Speak up before it's too late."

And then another man stepped around from the hallway. "It's already too late."

Blain!

"I'd suggest you two hand over that key," he said, his own gun drawn. "You're not getting the necklace and you are not getting away with anything else. But you are going to jail for murder."

Althea looked shocked. "How did he get in, Victor? You told me he'd be taken care of." Her skin turned a molten pink. "We have to end this. Go talk to your mother and get her to be reasonable."

Santo held up a hand. "No one is going to disturb our parents. You had your chance."

Victor drew a weapon and stepped up beside Althea. "Everything will work out." Holding the gun on Santo and Blain, he tugged Althea away. "Let's get out of here."

"No." Althea yanked at Rikki and tugged her back, her gun held to Rikki's head. She gave Blain a cold stare. "Put that gun down or I'll take her out of here and none of you will see her alive again."

"You won't do that," Blain said, his gun still raised. "You need Rikki to show you where the jewelry is hidden. Tell her, Santo."

Santo nodded, his hands in the air. "I know

exactly where it's located. If you want that necklace so badly, well, I'll be glad to give it to you."

"I'll kill her after I find the box," Althea said, bobbing her head. "I don't need you anymore, Santo. We'll get the necklace and then Victor and I can finally leave together just as we planned."

Santo started toward them again, his dark eyes on Victor, his shaggy black hair ruffled. "My own brother, double-crossing me. Victor, you know you won't get away with this."

Victor didn't seem to care. He looked gaunt and tired, his brown eyes flashing. "Don't be stupid, brother. Your wife wants to be with me."

Rikki wondered why Victor seemed so detached and uncaring. He looked so different, too. His hair was shaved short. He'd aged into someone she didn't recognize. Had Victor truly lost his mind?

Blain tried to make a move, but Althea waved her gun again. "I said, drop the gun. I can always kill her now. I'll find the necklace on my own if I have to." She edged the gun closer to Rikki. "And if you come after us, I will kill her just like I killed Tessa and that idiot Chad."

Rikki tried to twist away but Althea held her. Rikki watched Blain, her gaze holding his. He didn't want her to try anything that could result in a shoot-out.

Blain held up one hand and then placed his

gun onto the floor but shook his head. "You don't need to kill anyone else. We can work this out. Take me and I'll find the box you're looking for. I think it's hidden underneath the floor in the office."

Althea let out a cackle. "Everyone is so noble today. Take me. No, take me." She gave Santo a look of disdain and then shook her head at Blain. "I can't do that." She turned the gun toward Blain but Santo pushed Blain out of the way.

And then a shot rang out and Rikki watched as Santo stumbled to the floor.

"No," she screamed as Victor grabbed her and forced her toward the office while Althea held the gun on Blain.

"Don't do it," Blain said. "You'll regret this."

"I only regret that I married the wrong Alvanetti," Althea said. "I have the key and I'm leaving here with her. I don't care what Sonia or anyone else says. Rikki knows where that box is. She has to know. I've searched everywhere. She'll inherit the necklace but it should have been ours." She stared down at where Santo held his shoulder. "I need that necklace."

Then she shot the gun into the air and pushed Rikki up the hallway. "Don't follow us," she said to Blain.

Rikki glanced back, worried about Santo and

afraid that Blain would be shot next. When her eyes met Blain's he nodded to her. "I'm going to come for you, Rikki. I promise."

But after Victor slammed the door to the hall-way and locked it, she had to wonder if he'd be able to keep that promise.

Blain stooped to check on Santo.

"Go, go," Santo said. "I'll be okay."

Sam Kent came running from the back of the warehouse. "Hey, everybody okay here?"

"Check on Santo," Blain called. "He's been shot. They took Rikki."

"They won't get far," Sam shouted. "We've got people on the way."

"I'm going after them. They're headed to the office."

"Got it," Sam called. "Be careful, son."

Blain rushed outside, hoping to ambush them at the front of the big building. The dark, moon-less night was draped in a heavy humidity that chilled him down to his bones. The parking area was empty now, except for the dark SUV hidden out back. His dad had parked on the road. Billy Rogers was handcuffed in the backseat.

Blain prayed their little sting wouldn't get Rikki killed.

Things had gone down fast after Billy Rogers told them the plan. Blain and his dad had decided to hurry out to the warehouse and wait for Victor and Althea, but Blain had called Santo to warn him. Good thing, too. Victor and Althea had detoured to Rikki's town house, giving Blain just enough time to get everyone situated here and warn the Alvanettis to be on the lookout. Blain should have taken them both out the minute they arrived but Santo thought he could reason with them.

Now Rikki was at the mercy of her brother and the mastermind behind this heist—Althea Alvanetti. He'd have to sort all of this out later. He had to help Rikki.

He approached the hulking building from the side, a sick kind of dread filling his heart. The door was locked tight and after checking several windows and doors, Blain decided the place was empty.

Where had they taken Rikki?

Rikki didn't know where she was.

They found the secret compartment hidden beneath a rug under the desk. Victor lifted out a heavy wooden box that looked like a true treasure chest. Then Althea insisted on hurrying toward an underground storage area.

"We need to get out of here," she kept shouting. "And we need to kill her and dump her."

Victor finally showed some emotion. "I'm not

killing my sister. Do you want to spend the rest of your life in jail?"

"We can kill her and go away, Victor. To anywhere in the world. They can't find us now. Tessa is dead. Chad is dead. We're free and clear now." Then she snorted. "Except for this one little detail—your sister." When he didn't make a move, Althea added, "Do I need to remind you that I have certain information that can ruin you forever?"

Rikki didn't dare speak up for fear that Althea would realize she'd blurted out too much information. But she now saw the truth. Althea was blackmailing Victor.

But Victor didn't seem too worried about that. "You shouldn't have shot the woman, Althea. You know what Rikki looks like. How could you have mistaken Tessa for my sister?"

Althea urged him on, her gun pressing in Rikki's back and they climbed down a set of stairs. "I haven't seen your dear sister since the wedding last year. I panicked, okay. It was an accident."

Victor let out a grunt of frustration and lifted the box onto an old table. "All because of the infamous wedding where you overheard Sonia talking to me about the necklace. Rikki stood to inherit it and you didn't like that."

"It wasn't right." Rikki heard Althea shuffling

behind her. "I'd had it with Santo," Althea said. "And then your mother encouraged me to take matters into my own hands."

"Yes, she sure did." Victor sounded defeated. "But I don't think she meant for you to kill anyone or steal a priceless necklace. She wanted you to save your marriage."

They discussed and argued until all of the pieces of the puzzle fell into place. Rikki stayed quiet until they'd moved deep into the underground storage area that sat near the river. The plastic curtains to the loading dock flapped in a slow breeze. She thought she heard water lapping against a shore.

The wind surrounded her while they dragged her toward the big open doors. This part of the building smelled musty and decayed. She didn't want to think about what they planned to do to her.

"Do you think this will work?" Althea asked.

"It's the only way," Victor replied. "You're more stealthy and athletic than me. And I believe you know these particular woods. You can make it out with the necklace and I'll take care of everything else."

"I want to see it first," Althea said, her tone full of a greedy urgency. "We need to check the box."

Rikki absorbed everything. Could they be

near the woods where Althea must have hidden the night she shot Tessa?

"Let's hurry," Victor said on a breath of irritation. "Detective Kent confirmed what we already knew."

Althea groaned. "Your father walked in last time and caught me. Then that stupid Chad Presley showed up."

Rikki gulped a breath. "Did you kill Chad, Althea?"

"Shut up," Althea said, yanking out an ornate key. "I had no choice. He showed up to talk to dear old dad about you, the idiot. He was worried about you after he heard about Tessa's tragic murder."

Rikki blinked back tears. Chad hadn't come here to kill her. He'd only wanted to talk to her father.

"And I guess you had no choice when you killed Tessa, either," Rikki shouted, bile rising in her throat.

"She got in the way," Althea said. "It's a shame. I planned to kill you but your friend showed up before I could find that infernal key. I had to run before you saw me. Then Victor talked me out of it but now—"

Rikki didn't care if she lived or died now that she knew the truth. "Victor, please stop this now. Stop before it's too late."

Althea cackled. "It's already too late for you. I have the key and I have everything I need now."

Rikki started to retort but Victor's hand grasped hers and squeezed tight. A warning? He must have purposely forced Althea to talk. He'd given Rikki all the information she needed. Was he going to help her, after all?

She stood silent while Althea held the ornate key that Sonia had apparently hidden in Rikki's purse on the day of the wedding. Victor didn't make a move.

Althea chuckled when the big heavy box clicked open. "Let's see what we have." She stared down and then let out a yell. "What is this?"

Victor walked over and shone a flashlight on the deep box. "It looks like trinkets."

Althea slammed her hands against the old table. "It's junk, Victor. Junk. It's like kids' toys." She turned on Rikki. "Where is the necklace?"

Rikki went on instinct after remembering something her mother had said. "I'm tired of lying. It's at the house. But you'd better hurry. Detective Kent will send out a search party."

She watched Althea pacing around, her hand pulling through her short, spiky hair, her eyes going wild and unsure.

And in that brief moment, Victor leaned close. "I'll explain later, Rikki, but… I'm not a part of this. I'm going to get you out of here."

TWENTY-ONE

Althea pulled Rikki away from Victor. "I don't like being double-crossed. I want that necklace!"

Althea was beyond reason. She lunged at Victor and knocked him against the wall. He hit his head on the corner of an iron shelf.

Rikki screamed and pushed at Althea. The other woman came at her but Althea didn't have her gun. She'd laid it on the table by the old box. Rikki kicked at Althea and pushed her toward Victor. He stumbled to his feet and grabbed Althea and held her while Rikki reached for the gun.

Althea screamed and shoved at Victor. Still disoriented, he called out to Rikki. "Get out of here. Run."

"I won't leave you," Rikki shouted.

Althea broke loose and rushed toward her. Rikki screamed and held to the gun but Althea was taller and stronger. She lifted Rikki's hand up in the air and tried to pry the gun away from her.

Victor moved toward them. "Stop it, Althea. It's over." He held his head and then he sank to the floor and passed out.

Althea screamed and bent Rikki back against the table. "No. No. I won't let it be over. We need the money. I have to get away from this family, from this place."

Rikki stared into the eyes of a madwoman and sent up a prayer that if Althea killed her, the death would be quick. She groaned and used every ounce of her being to stop Althea.

Then she heard footsteps echoing down the stairs. "Rikki?

She took in air and tried to call out. "Blain, down here!"

But it was too late. Althea held Rikki pinned to the table and wrestled the gun closer and closer to Rikki's midsection.

Blain called out. "Let her go. Now!"

Althea didn't seem to hear him. But Rikki had a reason to fight now. Blain had given her so many reasons to live. She grunted and with one last surge of energy she kicked and lifted her body enough to force Althea up.

"Let her go," Blain shouted.

Althea turned then, the gun aimed at Blain. He lifted his gun and shot at her several times.

Althea fell to the floor and went still while Rikki stood against the table, the horror of the situation causing her to gulp and hold her hands to her face.

And then, the room went quiet and she was in Blain's arms.

Safe, warm and treasured.

Treasured.

"It's over," he said, his hands tangled in her hair. "It's all right now, Rikki."

Franco Alvanetti sat in the big chair behind his desk and stared over at Blain and Rikki. "I can't believe what you're telling me. Both of my sons in the hospital and my daughter-in-law dead. All because of a necklace."

Blain nodded. "All because of a necklace and a myth regarding some sort of ill-gained treasure."

Franco wiped at his eyes and looked over at Rikki. "We can't let your mother hear about this. It will destroy her."

Rikki swallowed and glanced at Blain. "But Althea indicated that Mama might know something more. That Mama encouraged her to…take matters into her own hands."

"Your mother was probably telling Althea to save her marriage. Althea always did love the money more than she loved your brother."

"That is so true."

They all turned to find Sonia in a wheelchair being pushed by Peggy and Daphne.

Franco got up and hurried to his wife. "What are you doing out of bed, Sonia?"

Sonia wiped at her eyes and waved the two nurses away. After they left, she said, "I know more about this than anyone. I hear things, see things, and I suppose I said things that didn't make sense but I was trying to save my family. I knew something was going on." She smiled at Rikki. "I tried to warn you but... I was all mixed up."

Rikki got up to kneel in front of her mother. "You mentioned the key and the Bible. But which key and which Bible, Mama?"

"I don't know," Sonia said. "I remember bits and pieces." She glanced around. "It started after your cousin's wedding. I went on my Mediterranean cruise and met up with Victor. He told me that Althea had tried to have an affair with him. She wanted to leave Santo and move to Europe."

"That's crazy," Franco said, sitting down on a bench next to Sonia. "Victor never liked her."

"She told him what she'd heard at the wedding. Me, telling Victor about the diamond-and-emerald necklace. I'd already told Santo that if anything happened to me, I wanted Rikki to have it." She shrugged. "He might have told

Althea or he might have forgotten. He never really listens to me, anyway."

Franco went pale. "You mean the necklace I gave you when Rikki was born? Is that the necklace Althea wanted?"

Sonia nodded. "I hid it. I was afraid of it. I was afraid of the treasure you purchased all those years ago. That somehow that treasure would be the ruin of us one day."

Franco let out a sigh and explained. "I bought it from a treasure hunter and convinced him to sell it to me at a cut-rate price. But I sold off everything but the necklace. That treasure helped us to launch our business." He gave his wife a sad stare. "I'm not proud of how I forced that poor man to cut that deal but... I can't go back and change it now."

"Althea overheard Mama talking about it and she approached Victor and forced him into a plan to help her steal it," Rikki said. "I finally figured that part out when they took me inside the warehouse. Althea was blackmailing Victor. She has something on him."

"Victor wouldn't do this," Sonia said. "He's made some mistakes but he was trying to clean himself up. Both of our boys want to do what's right, Franco."

Franco patted her hand. "I know, darling. And I promised you the same." He looked at Blain.

"I went legitimate years ago thanks to your dad, Detective Kent. He gave me a chance to make things right and I tried my best to do that. For my wife and for our baby daughter. And because Sonia taught me to be faithful in God's plan, not my own." He stared out at the water. "I've failed miserably."

Rikki wiped at her eyes. "Victor was trying to protect me. But why didn't he come forward sooner?"

Both of her brothers walked into the room. Santo had his right arm in a sling, his upper arm bandaged. Victor followed, looking pale, his head bandaged.

"We broke out of the hospital," Santo said. "I want to see my children."

"They're fine," Franco said. "Peggy is with them. You can see them after we get to the bottom of this mess."

Santo kissed his mother. "I'm so sorry, Mama."

Victor glanced at Rikki. "I had to pretend to help her. I sent Mama home after she became ill but I worried that Althea would do Mama harm so I kept trying to distract her by pretending to go along with her crazy plan. I told Santo what was going on but—"

"I didn't want to listen," Santo said. "I couldn't believe my wife could be so conniving and callous."

"We fought about it for months," Victor said, "but when she killed your friend, I had to follow through. She found out about some items I smuggled and she held it over my head. I had to come back home and try to stop her."

"But I got shot at," Rikki said, trying to fathom his reasoning. "Someone killed one of the guards."

"Althea's doings," Victor said. "She hired John Darty. But Althea shot Tessa, thinking she was you. Your friend tried to leave a clue. That wasn't my initial. It was probably an A."

"For Althea," Rikki said. "We couldn't figure it out."

"And the night we got chased on the bay road?" Blain asked.

"Billy Rogers was working undercover," Victor said. "And so was I. I had to pretend to keep her calm so we tried to scare you. We never intended to send you over the bluffs.

"When Althea left Santo, I was afraid she'd gone off the deep end. But we met in Miami and then I came back here with her. I agreed to help bring her in, in exchange for…a lighter sentence. We had to make it look like we'd tried to scare you, Rikki."

"You did," Rikki said. "A dangerous game, Victor."

"I'm sorry I let it go so far," Victor replied. "So sorry."

Santo nodded, his eyes full of fatigue. "I feel the same. Now I have to tell my children that their mother is dead."

"She was unstable," Sonia said. "I knew it, too. I tried to encourage her but she misunderstood my intentions."

"She said you were in charge of this family," Rikki replied.

"I am," Sonia said on a smile. "But in a good way."

"I can vouch for that," Franco said. Then he turned to Rikki. "I need to clarify one more thing, however. Drake's accident—"

"Was just that," Rikki said. "I have to believe that or all of this has been in vain." She glanced around. "And I have to accept that sometimes, things just aren't what they seem."

"Not what they seem." Sonia glanced around the room and then let out a gasp. "I remembered. I just remembered." She pointed to the bookshelf behind Franco's desk. "The big Bible up there. Would someone please get it down for me?"

Blain hurried to lift the ornate Bible off the shelf.

He placed it on the desk. "Do we need the key?"

Rikki pulled out the key Althea had used back at the warehouse. "Will this one work?"

Victor nodded. "The fake box was never

locked. It had a latch that easily opened. Althea never even noticed when she used the key."

"I found it on the floor," Rikki explained. "It should be evidence, right, Blain?"

He smiled at that. "You've learned a lot, hanging with me."

"Open it," Sonia said, a bittersweet smile on her face.

Blain turned the key in the big lock that held the Bible closed. When he opened the Bible, he found a secret compartment inside. Rikki reached in and pulled out the necklace.

She looked at Blain and then held the intricate necklace up. A diamond-encrusted chain held an inch-wide emerald-and-diamond teardrop necklace that shimmered in the early morning light.

"This has to be worth millions," she said.

"It is," Franco replied. "Sonia hid it because she was afraid it would only bring her heartache." He touched a hand to his wife's shoulder. "And I never even knew it was here."

"You should read your Bible more often," Sonia said to her husband, her old brilliant smile lighting up the room. "I always told all of you that."

Franco kissed her. "Don't get sick again, darling. I'll read the scriptures to you every night, I promise."

"I'm better now," Sonia promised. "But I

wanted you to have the necklace, Rikki. Your father changed after you were born."

"We've all changed," Santo said. "But we've paid a heavy price. I don't want any part of that necklace."

"I hope you all can forgive me," Victor said. He stared at Blain. "I know I gave a statement the other night and I understand I can only hope for a short prison sentence or at the least, probation. But I've kept records and I have taped conversations to prove that Althea planned most of this." He looked at Rikki. "I only wish I'd stopped it sooner."

Blain rubbed his forehead. "We'll have to sort it all out, but I think we can safely say that this case is closed. We've matched the partial shoe prints to Althea's sneakers and along with Billy Rogers's statement and Althea's jumbled confession to Rikki, I think we're okay."

Sonia cried and hugged everyone. Blain bagged the necklace as evidence. Then Sonia said, "I have a splendid idea. Why don't we donate this to Alec Caldwell's next fund-raiser for the Alexander and Vivian Caldwell Canines Service Dog Training Facility? I can't think of a better way to make this completely right."

Blain leaned close to Rikki. "I can think of a few other ways to make this right."

"Such as?" she asked, her heart hopeful for the first time in weeks.

"Attend Alec and Marla's wedding with me and then we'll celebrate Christmas together."

"I like that idea," she said. They waited until her brothers and her parents had left for breakfast. Finally, they were alone in the office.

Blain pulled her in his arms. "I don't know where we're going from here, but I want you in my life, Rikki. Do you think we can make it?"

Rikki tugged him close. "I think we have a good chance. We've survived the worst and we were both wrong about so many things."

"Let's make a new start," he said. "After all, this is a special time of year."

She stared down at the sparkling necklace. "Yes, and we both know what the real treasure is, don't we?"

"Yes, we do," he said.

Blain leaned close and kissed her. "Merry Christmas, Rikki."

"Merry Christmas," Rikki said. She kissed Blain and held him close, a sweet peace settling over her. She had so much to be thankful for.

Together they went into the big den where her family had gathered by the Christmas tree.

And she thanked God for a chance to start over again.

One week later
Christmas Eve

"This was such a lovely wedding," Sonia said, all bundled up in her big evening coat. "Thank you, Hattie, for inviting our family."

Alec's jovial aunt Hattie held her hand against her baby-blue cape and patted Sonia on the hand. "It was our pleasure. I understand you need to get home, but I'll come out and visit soon."

Sonia nodded and reached up from her wheelchair to take Rikki's hand. "Bring Blain back to the house for cookies and punch tonight, darling."

Rikki kissed her mother and watched her parents leave through the open garden gate. "Well, at least we didn't manage to distract attention from the bride. Marla looks so pretty."

The bride wore a white lacy dress with a white long-sleeved lacy bolero over it and the groom wore a tuxedo. The big outdoor fireplace, along with smaller fire pits and heaters set in discreet locations around the yard, kept everyone warm but the evening had turned out to be mild, anyway.

Rikki looked over to where Marla and Alec were dancing on the makeshift floor that had been set up underneath twinkling lights in the big garden of Caldwell House. The white

Victorian mansion had been decorated to the hilt with red and white bows, white and red flowers of all kinds, several different decorated Christmas trees, and more white lights. "This place looks like a big wedding cake."

"Yes, and I hear Marla baked her own cake," Blain said. "Let's go try a piece."

"It does look good." Five white tiers covered with creamy eatable magnolias and bright red ganache poinsettias. "And they look happy."

"I'm happy myself." She loved Blain in a tuxedo, loved watching him stand as Alec's best man.

He smiled over at her and took her hand. "Before we have cake, let's dance. You know, we've never danced together."

"We have a lot of firsts to get through," Rikki said.

"And a lifetime to try them all over and over again."

Rikki looked into his eyes. "So do you want that?"

He pulled her into his arms and they started waltzing to the soft music. "A lifetime with you? Yes, I do. I love you in this amazing green dress and I love that little black furry muff around your shoulders and… I love your eyes, your pretty lips." He stopped. "I love you, Rikki."

"I love you, too," she said. "But my family—"

"Will now have a police officer hanging around."

"I think we can all live with that," she said. "I know we still have a lot to work through but I think we're on the right path now."

Then she kissed him and smiled up at him. "I'm coming home, Blain. To you."

* * * * *

Dear Reader,

How far would you go to protect someone in your family?

That was the question when I came up with the idea for this book. Rikki Alvanetti left her home because she believed her family was involved in criminal activity. She thought they'd had her young husband killed. But when she comes home due to her mother's illness and other issues, she begins to see her powerful family in a new light.

Blain Kent doesn't trust anyone in the Alvanetti family, but as a detective, he has to keep an eye on them. When Rikki is forced to turn to him for help after her best friend is murdered in Rikki's town house, he doesn't know who she really is. When he discovers her true identity, he certainly can't trust her.

But these two adversaries are drawn together in spite of their difference. Blain and Rikki realize that sometimes things aren't as they seem and that the worst of enemies can turn out to be the closest of allies.

I hope this story entertained you and that it made you stop and think about people in your life who might seem untrustworthy or questionable. Mother Teresa said if we are busy loving people we don't have time to judge them. I para-phrased her words, but the meaning is clear. We have to peel back the layers and find the truth, good or bad.

I invite you to watch for Preacher Rory's story. He is the next hero of the Men of Millbrook Lake.

Until next time—

May the angels watch over you. Always.

Lenora Worth

LARGER-PRINT BOOKS!

**GET 2 FREE
LARGER-PRINT NOVELS
PLUS 2 FREE
MYSTERY GIFTS**

Love Inspired®
SUSPENSE
RIVETING INSPIRATIONAL ROMANCE

Larger-print novels are now available...

YES! Please send me 2 FREE LARGER-PRINT Love Inspired® Suspense novels and my 2 FREE mystery gifts (gifts are worth about $10). After receiving them, if I don't wish to receive any more books, I can return the shipping statement marked "cancel." If I don't cancel, I will receive 4 brand-new novels every month and be billed just $5.49 per book in the U.S. or $5.99 per book in Canada. That's a savings of at least 19% off the cover price. It's quite a bargain! Shipping and handling is just 50¢ per book in the U.S. and 75¢ per book in Canada.* I understand that accepting the 2 free books and gifts places me under no obligation to buy anything. I can always return a shipment and cancel at any time. Even if I never buy another book, the two free books and gifts are mine to keep forever.

110/310 IDN GH6P

Name _____ (PLEASE PRINT) _____

Address _____ Apt. # _____

City _____ State/Prov. _____ Zip/Postal Code _____

Signature (if under 18, a parent or guardian must sign)

Mail to the **Reader Service:**
IN U.S.A.: P.O. Box 1867, Buffalo, NY 14240-1867
IN CANADA: P.O. Box 609, Fort Erie, Ontario L2A 5X3

**Are you a current subscriber to Love Inspired® Suspense books
and want to receive the larger-print edition?
Call 1-800-873-8635 or visit www.ReaderService.com.**

* Terms and prices subject to change without notice. Prices do not include applicable taxes. Sales tax applicable in N.Y. Canadian residents will be charged applicable taxes. Offer not valid in Quebec. This offer is limited to one order per household. Not valid for current subscribers to Love Inspired Suspense larger-print books. All orders subject to credit approval. Credit or debit balances in a customer's account(s) may be offset by any other outstanding balance owed by or to the customer. Please allow 4 to 6 weeks for delivery. Offer available while quantities last.

Your Privacy—The Reader Service is committed to protecting your privacy. Our Privacy Policy is available online at www.ReaderService.com or upon request from the Reader Service.

We make a portion of our mailing list available to reputable third parties that offer products we believe may interest you. If you prefer that we not exchange your name with third parties, or if you wish to clarify or modify your communication preferences, please visit us at www.ReaderService.com/consumerchoice or write to us at Reader Service Preference Service, P.O. Box 9062, Buffalo, NY 14240-9062. Include your complete name and address.